THE MAN WHO WAS TWISTED BUT HIP

CRAIG STEPHEN COPLAND

The Man Who Was Twisted But Hip

Note to Readers:

Your enjoyment of this new Sherlock Holmes mystery will be enhanced by re-reading the original story that inspired this one –
The Man with the Twisted Lip.
It has been appended and may be found in the back portion of this book.

The Man Who Was Twisted But Hip

A New Sherlock Holmes Mystery #8

Craig Stephen Copland

Published by:

Conservative Growth Inc.
3104 30th Avenue, Suite 427
Vernon, British Columbia, Canada
V1T 9M9

Cover design by Rita Toews.

ISBN: 1507650949
ISBN-13: 9781507650943

Dedication

To those courageous men and women throughout the world, Jew and Gentile alike, who have fought against the evil of anti-Semitism.

Welcome to New Sherlock Holmes Mysteries -

"The best-selling series of new Sherlock Holmes stories. All faithful to The Canon."

Each story is a tribute to one of the sixty original stories about the world's most famous detective. If you are encountering these new stories for the first time, start with *Studying Scarlet,* and keep going. (https://www.amazon.com/dp/B07CW3C9YZ)

If you subscribe to Kindle Unlimited, then you can 'borrow for free' every one of the books.

They are all available as ebooks, paperbacks, hardcovers, and in large print.

Check them out at www.SherlockHolmesMysteries.com.

NEW SHERLOCK HOLMES MYSTERIES
WWW.SHERLOCKHOLMESMYSTERY.COM

Contents

Acknowledgments

This novella, a pastiche Sherlock Holmes story, was inspired *The Man With The Twisted Lip* by Arthur Conan Doyle; by *The Hunchback of Notre Dame,* by Victor Hugo; and by *J'accuse,* by Émile Zola. All three of these writers are among the greats of western literature. I am indebted to them.

My dearest and best friend, Mary Engelking, read all drafts, helped with whatever historical and geographical accuracy was required, and offered insightful recommendations for changes to the narrative structure, characters, and dialogue. Thank you.

The Downtown Oakville Writers' Group has endured drafts of my Sherlock Holmes stories and made innumerable useful recommendations for improvement. Thank you.

Many words and whole phrases and sentences have been lifted and copied shamelessly and joyfully from the sacred canon of Sherlockian literature and a few from Victor Hugo.

.

Chapter One

At the Union Hall

My nephew, Isaac Whitney, was a good lad. The death of his father while he was still a callow young man had left a great void in his life, and he sought to fill the emptiness by devoting his time and passions to one popular enthusiasm after another — practices that were easy to attain and just as easy to get rid of. For a while, he joined the bicycle craze that had swept the country, and every weekend he and a band of young men and women would take to the roads on two-wheelers laden with picnic baskets, and engage in vigorous physical outings in nature. The guardians of proper English society condemned this popular fad noting that while it might be a good form of physical exercise for young men, it was entirely inappropriate for young women. The constant movement of their limbs and the exertion of their bodies obviously encouraged the liberation of their animal spirits, as evidenced by their flushed faces, perspiring brows, and loud exclamations.

As the bicycle craze faded, so did Isaac's interest in it, and he replaced it with the next nonsensical fad to come along, the playing of board games.

That frivolous passion understandably did not last long and was overtaken by his conversion to Theosophy. For many evenings on end, he would meet with other devotees and read and debate the finer points of the sermons and writings of such luminaries as Madame Blavatsky and Mrs. Annie Besant. For a week or two, he proclaimed that he was going to travel to Madras so that he could immerse himself in the unexplained laws of nature and the powers latent in man. This plan soon vanished once he contemplated the cost and realized that he had not sufficient funds to get himself to Brighton, let alone to the sub-continent. But some of the practitioners of Theosophy were good friends with the Fabians, and so Isaac sought to join their activities, which in turn led to his latest obsession — the radical overthrow of the capitalist order and seizing of the means of production by the proletariat. I did not think for a moment that he had any comprehension of the meaning of dialectic materialism, but what did that matter when a young man is able to submerge the pain of a lost father and leap out of bed every morning to join his comrades as they marched out to save the world.

His mother, my dear sister-in-law Mrs. Kate Whitney, was distressed by his most recent obsession and complained about it whenever she came to visit my wife Mary (née Morstan) and me. I listened patiently and then tried to reassure her with the wise saying: that any man who was not a radical when he was twenty had no heart, and if he was still a radical when he was forty, he had no head. She did not appear to be enamored with the prospect of waiting for another twenty years for her boy to put away childish things.

Such was the state of affairs on a Saturday morning in the spring of 1897. Mary and I were in our cheery sitting-room enjoying a breakfast cup of tea when there came a ring to my bell.

"A patient," said Mary laying down her needle-work. "And on a Saturday morning. It must be serious. English people never become ill on a weekend. You'll have to go out."

Yet it was not a patient at all. A woman, clad in some dark-colored stuff, with a black veil, entered the room. It was my sister-in-law, Mrs. Kate Whitney. Why she insisted on dressing like a widow six years after the death of her husband was beyond all understanding, except, of course, that our dear Queen Victoria was still doing the same thing forty years after the death of Albert.

She rushed up to Mary and threw her arms around her neck and began to sob.

"Oh. I am so frightened. He hasn't been home for the past two nights. I am worried sick," she said in between whimpers. "I am so sorry to intrude on your weekend, but I am at my wits' end. I don't know what to do."

"Sister, dear. It is quite all right," said my wife, who truly had the gift of consolation for the afflicted and who attracted such needy souls to her like birds to a lighthouse. "Sit down and have some wine and water. Or would you prefer a cup of tea? And tell us all about it."

Mrs. Whitney sat down by the hearth, and after warming her hands, she lifted her veil and took up a magazine and used it to fan her face. Then she lifted the fresh cup of tea and, between some bites of biscuit, sipped slowly on it. Having finished her refreshment, she recommenced her sobs. "Isaac has not been home for the past two nights," she said, covering her face with her hands but opening her palms sufficiently for her words to be heard clearly. "On Thursday evening, he told me he was off to yet another meeting of those radicals he has been consorting with. I have not seen hide or hair of him since."

Here she put down the cup of tea and leaned forward in her chair. In *sotto voce,* she added, "It was held in the East End, in a union hall. I implored him not to go, but he spurned me, his mother, and he simply looked up to the sky and said, 'Our *fraternité* in France are fighting for liberty and the rights of man. I have no choice. Danger or no, I am called to stand with them'"

"Oh, my dear sister," said my wife. "That is terrible. He could have been beaten, or thrown in jail, or worse. No wonder you are so upset."

"It is worse. He has no money for food. He will have missed his supper last night and will be famished. He becomes so unhappy when he has not eaten properly. It breaks my heart to think of him suffering so. But I don't know what to do. I would go and fetch him, but I have never in my entire life been east of Aldgate. It would be entirely a foreign country to me. I might as well be in the Congo."

I could see the inevitable direction of this conversation and resigned myself to losing an otherwise vacant Saturday morning. "Oh, please, Kate. Do not fret. I will come with you, and we will find him and bring him home." Having said this, I reconsidered, realizing that the only prospect worse than giving up my morning would be spending the next three hours gadding about London with my sister-in-law. I could manage it much better if I were alone.

"Better still," I said. "I will go on my own. You just stay here and enjoy the morning with Mary. I'll have the lad back in time for a nourishing lunch."

"Oh no, you really do not have to put yourself out. Oh, but how can I thank you enough? Mary is so blessed to have such a caring husband. Here, I have the address in my purse of the union hall." Again she dropped her voice as she uttered the words "union hall."

I rose and retired to dress. I could not possibly attire myself as a gentleman and still attend a meeting in a union hall, so I pulled on a heavy sweater, a pair of corduroy breeches, and my hiking boots. Then from the back of the wardrobe, I extracted an old riding jacket and an alpine hat. My dear wife accompanied me to the door.

"Darling," she said. "You are devilishly manly when all dressed up to go fly-fishing. Enjoy your outing." She gave me a kiss on the cheek and a pat on my bottom and closed the door behind me.

I hailed a hansom on Marylebone Road and gave the driver the address. He gave me a queer look up and down and headed east. There was no great difficulty in the first stage of my adventure. It was a clear, crisp spring morning, and I soon had thrown open the window of the cab and repeated the words of Browning, "Oh to be in England now that April's there." I couldn't remember any more of it, but that was enough to cheer my spirits all the way to Limehouse.

The Bar of Gold union hall was a plain red brick building squeezed between a slop-shop and a gin-shop. A gaggle of dockworkers were standing around the entrance, smoking cheap smelling cigarettes. I walked past them and approached the hall. My way was blocked by a Dane and a Lascar, guarding the entrance.

"You look," said the Dane, "like you are going fishing, sir, not to a meeting here."

"That is what my wife thought as well. It worked to fool her," I responded with a laugh and gave him a pat on the shoulder. He laughed in return and bade me enter.

On looking at the hall, I thought for a moment that I was surveying a battlefield the day after the bombardment, except that there was no blood. Lying in fantastic poses and in various places around the floor were men in workman's coats as if all had fallen after the burst of an artillery shell. Some were snoring loudly. The place stank of stale ale and cheap tobacco, and the universal odor of young male bodies who have not bathed. A few chaps were standing and drinking their morning tea, and I could not help but be amused looking at them. Everyone was wearing a short, heavy blue coat with a scarf curled with careful carelessness around their necks. Most were wearing tams on their heads rather than a working man's cap. They had all studiously washed and ruffled their hair and looked so very French. Of course, they were all speaking English, and I was reasonably certain that not one of them knew a word of the Gallic tongue beyond *oui* and *non*. On the far side of the hall, huddled amongst the ruffians by a small brazier of burning charcoal, and sipping his tea, was my nephew.

"Good morning, Isaac," I said. He looked up at me with a perplexed expression.

"Good morning, Uncle James," he replied. My Christian name is not James but John. However, he had two other uncles on his father's who were also named John, and his mother had decided that it would be too confusing for a child to have three Uncle John's, so she insisted on his calling me James, my second name. I thought that it would be too much for a young mind to bear only if he were an imbecile, but I held my tongue and went along with it.

"What are you doing here?" he asked in a somewhat dazed manner.

"You are supposed to be having lunch with your Aunt Mary, your mother and me, and your mother has sent me to fetch you. Please put down your tea and come along."

"Oh. I'm so sorry. I must have forgotten." He rose and pulled on his coat. "What's for lunch?"

I took him by the arm and led him towards the door. Before reaching it, my way was blocked by an elderly cripple. He had a large hump on his back and was bent over, leaning heavily on a cane as he hurriedly shuffled his way into my path.

"Excusez-moi, m'sieur," the twisted old fellow said. "Vous êtes a soldier of zee revolution? Oui? You are here aussi to donnez votre fraternité to zee struggle of zee French people against zair oppressors? Oui?"

"No, my good man. I am only here to fetch my nephew and bring him home. Now if you will excuse me, please."

With the hand that was not on the cane, he grabbed my arm and stuck to me like a leech all the way out of the building and onto the pavement.

"Ah, mais m'sieur. Zen your nephew, he ees a revolutionary. N'est pas?"

"I believe, my man, that all he is right now is hungry. Now if you will excuse me, this is our cab, and we have to be on our way."

Then to my surprise, the old man stood straight up to a height of over six feet and looked right at me.

"Very well then, Watson. Send that hungry lad home in the cab. It is quite propitious of you to turn up. I could use your help." Grinning at my surprise, was none other than Sherlock Holmes.

"Holmes! Good heavens. What are you doing here?"

"Supporting zee struggle of zee French people. Enough, I will explain as we ride. Tell your driver that you will not be back home until the supper hour."

"Holmes, please. Mary is expecting me for lunch . . ."

"And will be quite pleased if you do not show up. She married you, as they say, for better or worse but not for lunch. And you, my dear friend, will be infinitely relieved not to have to spend your Saturday with your relatives. Come along."

I could not argue with him. He was right. I could not wish anything better than to be associated with my friend in one of those singular adventures, which were the normal condition of his existence. So I put young Isaac into the cab, gave a note to the cabman, and followed Holmes around the block to a high dog-cart that he had rented. "Please take the reins," he said, "and cross the river at the Tower Bridge." He then doffed his shabby coat, peeled off his walrus mustache and bushy eyebrows, and from his hunchback — a canvas sack tied around his body — he brought out his overcoat and deer-stalker hat. I drove west until we came to the broad, balustrated Tower Bridge, crossed the murky Thames as it flowed sluggishly beneath us, and turned east.

"Very well then, Holmes. Again, why were you there, and where are we going?"

"We have a seven-mile drive before us, to Lee, in Kent. There is a new client there who requires my assistance." He said no more.

"You answered my second question, Holmes. I am still all in the dark on my first. Why were you there?"

For a minute or two, he ignored me and stared out at the passing buildings. "You would not believe me if I told you that I had added radical politics to my weaknesses. So very well, if you must know, and please my friend, no unnecessary jibes. It is a bit humbling. It is Mycroft's doing."

Chapter Two

Orders from Mycroft

He reached into his pocket and pulled out a telegram and handed it to me. It ran:

TO: SHERLOCK HOLMES, 221B BAKER STREET

FROM: MYCROFT HOLMES, WESTMINSTER.

INFILTRATE THE DREYFUSARDS WHO MEET IN LIMEHOUSE.

GO TO MRS. NEVILLE ST. CLAIR IN KENT AND OFFER YOUR SERVICES. SHE IS EXPECTING YOU BEFORE LUNCH ON SATURDAY.

I was tempted to laugh. Sherlock Holmes was no respecter of persons, and I had watched him rudely dismiss earls and dukes and even a royal or two. There was only one person in London who successfully ordered him around. It infuriated him that he was helpless but to obey the summons of his older brother, Mycroft. Readers of my accounts of the adventures of Sherlock Holmes will remember that Mycroft Holmes did not merely work for the British government, he *was* the British government. There was not an important file in the past forty years pertaining to any part of the

Empire that had not crossed his desk and been committed to his prodigious memory. He called on his younger brother's unique skills rarely, but when he did, it was for a matter of profound concern to the nation. His request was a command performance, and Sherlock Holmes showed up and did as he was told.

I enjoyed some silent amusement at my esteemed colleague's expense and acknowledged to myself that the morning had become infinitely less tedious than I had earlier feared.

The journey down the Thames Valley on a spring morning was more than pleasant. I drove the dog-cart while Holmes sat in silence, his head sunk upon his breast, and with the air of a man lost in thought. Somewhere past Dartford, Holmes rose from his seat and joined me at the front.

"You have a grand gift of silence, Watson," said he.

"I have learned the hard way that it is useless to demand information from you before you are willing to divulge," I said back, bluntly. "When I do, all I get for my troubles is riddles. So if you are ready to speak, please do. If not, I can exercise my gift."

"You are aware, I assume, that all of France has torn itself apart yet again. This time, it is over what they are calling the Dreyfus affair."

"I have seen some stories in *The Times* but cannot say that I have followed it closely. It hardly seems a concern of the English," I said.

"If this world were run by the principles of logic and science, it would not be. But sadly, the English people are driven by their passions, and what more attractive a cause to be passionate about than something happening to the French."

"We do have a bit of a history on that," I conceded. "But it cannot have become so dangerous an alliance as to involve Mycroft's office."

"Indeed, I would not have thought so. But apparently, it has, and he is sufficiently concerned about it, else he would never have demanded my services. All I can deduce at this time is that he must have it on reliable report that the situation over there could explode, and drag England into the French quagmire."

He said nothing more on that matter, and I concluded that indeed he did not know anything more.

"Very well then," I continued. "Who is this lady we are going to see, and how is she connected to the matter?"

"Does the name of her husband, Neville St. Clair, mean anything to you? No? Have you read the theater pages lately?"

I thought for a moment. I was a bit of a fan of the stage, my father having been a rather respected actor in his day. "Why yes! Isn't that the name of this new chap who is getting all the rave reviews from the critics? He has the role of Quasimodo in the Lyceum's new production of *Notre Dame de Paris*. Playing opposite Ellen Terry's Esmeralda, is he not? The whole West End is buzzing about him. My father, bless his soul, once played that very role. Mary is dying for me to take her to see it. I suppose I will have to sometime after Easter. But how does that fit in?"

"That I confess I do not know," Holmes replied. "My taste, as you know, in evening's entertainment runs more to the symphony, but I have done some investigating into Mr. St. Clair."

"Yes. Do not stop there, Holmes."

"He was born into a wealthy family in Chesterfield, but his father, a schoolmaster, moved the family to Cornwall. He did his studies and graduated with a double first from Cambridge, and has been gainfully if unremarkably employed since that time by Whitehall. His wife, who we shall meet shortly, is the daughter of a wealthy brewer, and they were married some seven years ago and now have two children and a small but pleasant estate, The Cedars they call it, in Kent."

"How did he end up in the theater? Those Whitehall chaps don't have enough personality to be accountants. They are hardly the type to be on stage and leaving audiences breathless."

"It is passing strange to me as well, and I have had to discipline myself from reaching too many theories before I have sufficient data.

To add to the strangeness, do you happen to know who had been contracted to play Quasimodo?"

"I haven't the foggiest."

"None other than Henry Irving."

"The actor who disappeared back around Michaelmas? That fellow?" I said.

"Yes. The greatest actor on our present stage," said Holmes.

Henry Irving was famous throughout London, having courageously lifted himself from the poverty of his birth in the western village of Keinton Mandeville, if I remembered correctly. His strange disappearance was a continuing mystery. He had not an enemy in the world, except for the theater critics, and one can only imagine his wanting to murder them rather than vice versa.

"After Mr. Irving vanished," continued Holmes, "Mr. Neville St. Clair auditioned for his role, having had no previous training or experience in the theater, and was awarded it. He has been enthralling audiences ever since. He appears to have had an undiscovered talent for the stage. He is presently in the West End, preparing for the matinee performance, something I would advise everyone to avoid as those performances invariably are ruined by screaming children who cannot distinguish between fantasy and reality. Nevertheless, his being there will give us more than sufficient time to converse with Mrs. St. Clair."

"And why is she asking for your services?"

"Somehow, she has convinced herself that there was something beyond strange going on with her husband, that she is in want of a consulting detective, and cannot dare divulge her concerns to her husband."

"Well, then she has the finest and most confidential detective in the country."

We pulled up in front of a large villa. It was neatly kept with lovely gardens in spring bloom, all decent and in order except for a collection of children's riding toys and other game pieces spread out in gleeful abandon on the verdant lawn. A stable boy dashed out and took the lead of the horse, and Holmes and I walked up the gravel drive to the door.

It opened, and a small blonde woman appeared and reached out her hand to greet us. I would have placed her at about thirty years of age and had to restrain from staring at her since she was exceptionally attractive. She was clad in some sort of *light masseline de soie* with a touch of fluffy pink chiffon at her neck and wrists. Even after having had two children, she had a trim and perfectly proportioned figure and, in spite of her small stature, gave the air of one who is confident and self-assured.

"Mr. Sherlock Holmes," she said, addressing my companion. "Welcome to The Cedars. It was very kind of you to give up a beautiful Saturday and come to see me. And your friend?" she said, turning to me. "Have you come to do some fishing?"

"Madam," said Holmes. "This is my colleague and trusted partner, Dr. John Watson. He has kindly, at the last moment, agreed to give up his day of angling and help me with this visit."

I felt my face becoming red and would have happily given Holmes a kick. I could tell that he was enjoying the situation at my expense.

Holmes would not let it go. "You may speak in front of him in complete confidence, and I assure you that the fish whose lives you are saving by your making use of his time this morning will be most grateful."

The lady of the house let out a spontaneous laugh, and I did likewise. It was so seldom that Sherlock Holmes made any effort at humor that I was compelled to enjoy it.

"Please, gentlemen," said Mrs. St. Clair. "Be seated in the parlor. You have had a long ride, and the least I can do is provide you with some tea and lunch. Please," she said, motioning towards a grouping of chairs around the hearth. I was interested to see some modern touches in an older home. On the wall were several paintings in the recent French style in which the artist, at least to my eye, seemed incapable of accurately representing a scene or person and just did suggestive smudges instead. Very confusing, but apparently it was all the rage in Paris. Very well, I thought. You can, after all, always count on things to be different in Paris.

A maid brought in some tea along with servings of cold goose, cheese, and hot soup, and for a few minutes, Holmes, ostensibly on my behalf, chatted about the fishing prospects in the region. I determined for certain to give him a kick all the way to Charing Cross as soon as we got back on the road to London. Then, as expected, he changed the subject to the matter at hand.

"Madam, as our time as well as yours is restricted, we must come to the reason for our visit. Could you please state your case, and do be as frank and precise as you possibly can."

Mrs. St. Clair put down her tea, clasped her hands in her lap, sat up in her chair, and looked directly at Sherlock Holmes. "Mr. Holmes, I fear that you might think me no more than a frivolous young wife and a victim of a silly female imagination, but I assure you that I am not hysterical nor given to fainting. I try as best I can to be rigorously logical and sensible, and I would not have asked to meet with you if it were not that I suspect that there is something seriously amiss in my husband's life."

"My dear Mrs. Neville," responded Holmes. "I have seen too much not to know that the impressions of a woman are more valuable than the conclusions of an analytical reasoner. The suspicions and intuitions of a wife are invariably well-founded, even if at the time they cannot be fully explained. You have my full attention and respect. Pray, proceed."

"Thank you, sir. My husband, Mr. Neville St. Clair, came from a Cornwall family, but in spite of that, he was a brilliant student, sat the Foreign Service exams, and had a very promising career at Whitehall. He had moved up steadily in responsibility and appeared to be considered as one of the up-and-comers. He was certain to be in a very senior position before he turned forty years of age. I am quite proud of him and very satisfied and grateful for our life together. We have a lovely home and have been blessed with two healthy children. I was very happy with our life, and I thought he was as well."

Here she paused and took a long sip on her cooling tea.

"All of that," she said, "came to a crashing end this past fifteenth of October."

Chapter Three

The Cedars in Kent

The lovely Mrs. St. Clair looked up from her tea and continued her story.

"It was a Monday, and he returned home from Whitehall in time to see the children off to bed, and we sat down to dinner together. Sometimes he seems distracted over dinner as he reflects on the events of the day at Whitehall, but that evening he was particularly engaged with me and very conversant, though looking back, I suspect he was making a deliberate effort to be so. As soon as we finished dessert, he rose up out of his chair and came over to mine. He lovingly tilted my head slightly back and kissed me most tenderly and then returned to his chair. He looked intently at me and said, and I believe these were his exact words, he said, 'My darling Amelia, I want to assure you that beyond any possible doubt I am lovingly devoted to you and the children, and there is nothing in this universe that will ever endanger that bond.'

"Here he paused, and I was very perplexed. The kiss had been very touching. However, I knew that he was preparing to make some sort of major announcement. I just looked at him and waited, and then he said, 'I must tell you that I am utterly dissatisfied with my employment, my career, my prospects, indeed every part of every day I spend at Whitehall. I am nothing but one more trousered ape toiling for the Empire. It is stifling. It is meaningless. It is deeply unfulfilling. It is beyond boring day after day.'

"Well, Mr. Holmes, as you must know, there are thousands of women whose husbands work for the government and who have been recipients of such declarations, so I was concerned for his sake, but not overly alarmed. My husband has an exceptional mind and is constantly seeking to improve it with ever more wide-ranging knowledge. Although he had never before complained of a lack of stimulation at Whitehall, indeed I would have thought quite the opposite, I could imagine that he had come to such a place as he had described. I was about to suggest a short vacation through the Mediterranean, perhaps even leaving the children with our families, but then he surprised me beyond belief with his next statement."

"Yes, madam," said Holmes. "And what was that?"

"He said, 'My darling, I confess to you that in the deepest part of my soul, I have always had a passion for the arts, and especially for the stage. Since I was a boy, I have dreamed of being an actor. I have smothered, indeed suffocated that burning urge up until now, but I can no longer keep it hidden. It is the truth and must out.'

"'Really, darling,' I said in response. This was all news to me as I had never seen any such inclination. We occasionally went to the theater but only at my urging and he was as like as not to fall asleep during the second act.

"'Yes, my dearest,' he continued. 'And I am going to do something about it. We have no worries concerning our financial affairs, so I have decided to change my career and follow my dreams. Today a call went out for auditions for the role of Quasimodo in the Lyceum's upcoming production, and I submitted my name. If I am successful in being awarded the part, then I will give my notice to Whitehall and spend the remainder of my working life in my true spiritual home, which is the stage.'

"There has always been a keen sympathy between my husband and me, and my first reaction, gentlemen, as I sure you will understand, was to laugh at such an unbelievable idea. But I held my tongue, remembering the advice that is given to all young wives that they must never ridicule their husband's dreams since they invariably return to their senses in due time. And my common sense told me that there was not a chance under heaven that he would win the audition, so what was the harm. So I smiled sweetly at him and said, 'Splendid, sweetheart. I shall be your most enthusiastic and adoring fan,' and then I stood and walked over to him and returned the loving kiss he had earlier given me. He smiled in return and became very amorous, and I congratulated myself on my very wise response to his announcement, thinking that nothing would come of it."

"Ah, but something did come of it," said Holmes.

"Yes, sir. It did. On that Friday, he came home all excited and announced that he had won the audition, that he had given his notice to the government, and that he was on his way to fulfilling his dreams. I was shocked and completely speechless. What I had considered to be beyond imagining, had actually taken place. I just blurted out something like, 'That's not possible, Neville! It is a prized part, and all the best actors in the West End were vying for it. How could they have given it to you? You are a mandarin, not an actor!' Now I know that a wife should never display a lack of confidence in her husband, but I could not help it. What I had just been told was utterly incomprehensible.

"But it was indeed the truth. Neville patiently explained that acting had always been in his soul and that as soon as he was on stage, he was freed of all of his inhibitions, and he, as he said, 'let loose' and let his soul escape. He *became* Quasimodo, and he won the part. And the next day there was the announcement in *The Times*. It reported his brilliant audition, and, being a newspaper, they had to add that part of the reason was the resemblance in both appearance and native West England accent to Henry Irving, the actor who was intended to have the role before his disappearance a few weeks earlier. I thought that a silly observation since the role required all sorts of hideous make-up, and speaking with a terrible impediment and a French accent, but you know how the Press are these days.

"I was surprised as well that Whitehall let him go with only one week's notice and even began to pay part of his pension to him. He then had two weeks of rehearsals when I hardly saw him at all, and following that, they held the opening night."

Here I interrupted, for I remembered reading about that night in *The Times*. "And it was a triumph. Brought down the house. It has become the hottest ticket in the West End, and your husband is the toast of the town. My congratulations."

"Yes. Exactly, doctor. I attended the opening night in fear and dread that Neville would give a dreadful performance, make a fool of himself, and be utterly crushed. For three hours, I sat in absolute disbelief as I watched him, all made-up in his hideous costume, what with his hunchback, and horrible wart over his eye, and his lip all twisted out of shape. He scampered and jumped around all over the sets. He gave the most powerful and moving speeches. His devotion to Esmeralda was heartbreaking. And at the end, when he lay down in the grave and died beside her, there was not a lady in the audience who was not in tears. Even most of the men were trying not to weep. It was such a moving play. I have watched it now over twenty times, and I am still moved every time."

"And has his change of life brought stress into yours?" asked Holmes.

She shook her beautiful head. "No. Not at all. I feared it would and that my life, which up to now has been the envy of any daughter of a merchant brewer, would vanish. But in truth, my life has turned into a fairy tale. We have been catapulted into the most glittering of theater and literary society. Neville has been lionized throughout London. We are invited to awfully elegant parties, and luncheons, and salons. I have met and conversed with Sarah Bernhardt, and several of the D'Oyly Cart family, and John Synge and Bernard Shaw from Dublin, and Mr. Bulwer-Lytton, the novelist, and ever Oscar Wilde has chatted with my husband on several occasions and with me twice. Many others have visited Neville at his dressing room after the final curtain and the removal of all his makeup and congratulated him. The Prince of Wales dropped by and introduced himself as "Bertie" and invited us up to Sandringham for a weekend in the summer. It has been a dream world."

"I gather then that your husband has included you in his newfound fame," said Holmes.

"Entirely, sir. He has urged me to come to as many performances as I can, and if there is to any sort of party after a show, he has insisted that I come up in time for the end of the performance so that I can accompany him. Why this very evening I will leave on the eight o'clock train so that I can be in the West End by the end of the play, and accompany him to a late dinner party in Mayfair. As he often does, he has booked us a room at one of the posh hotels. We stay in the loveliest suites with fresh flowers abounding. In the mornings, we have the most exquisite and, if I may be permitted to say, affectionate breakfasts, and we lazily enjoy ourselves while the rest of the world is having to go off to work or to church."

"Have you been met with hostility from any of the people you have met?" asked Holmes. "Have they treated you with respect?"

"Very much so," she replied. "I have no university schooling, of course, but I did attend a proper ladies' college, and I was determined to never be a boring wife for my husband, so every day of my life, while he is off working, I read and study. I hired my own tutor and have learned enough Greek and Latin to read some of the classics, at least the important ones. My husband kept all of his texts from Cambridge, and I have read every one of them, which was not all that difficult. We receive *The Times* every day, and I read it in its entirety. And so, to my surprise, when we have attended all these parties with all these admired people I have found that I not only know what they are talking about, but that I have my own opinions on the pressing topics of the day, and that I can defend them capably."

With this, Holmes looked in my direction, and I understood that it was now my role, as a doctor, to inquire into some of the more delicate matters that may bring conflict to a marriage.

"Forgive me, my lady," I said. "I have to ask some frank questions related to your marriage."

"Of course, doctor, ask away," she replied. "Let me save you the embarrassment. I suppose you want to know if I suspect that there is some other woman who has become romantically linked to my husband."

"Frankly, yes, madam," I replied in my most reassuring doctorly manner.

"If only it were that simple," she responded, "I would have no need of calling the two of you all the way to Kent. No. Not for an instant do I suspect anything of that sort. Neville is consistently affectionate and amorous towards me. In the mornings and afternoons, he is either with me, or in the library, or engaging with the children. They have so enjoyed having him around during the day, and he brings them dolls and packages of bricks to play with. He leaves only in time to get to the theater for his makeup preparation. He either rushes from the end of the performance to the station so he can be home by half-past midnight, or I meet him at the stage door, and we go off to a party. If he is ravishing some poor young actress, he must be doing it in the wings in between scenes while still in his revolting costume. In which case, I more pity the silly girl than fear her. But I jest. So, no doctor. There has not been a single sign of his straying from his marriage."

"Have there been arguments between the two of you," I continued. "Is there acrimony? Please be frank with us."

Here she smiled. "Yes, doctor. There are sparkling arguments several times a week. We receive two subscriptions to *The Economist,* and both of us read it from cover to cover, and then we engage in the most vigorous of debates over its stories. I take the role of Mr. Gladstone, and he becomes Mr. Disraeli, and we argue back and forth. It is a rollicking good match that both of us are eager to take up with each other, and it always ends in good-natured laughter and an affectionate embrace. So that is the extent of our conflict, sir."

"And, again, forgive my asking, but what about your own conjugal relationship? And please, I am a doctor, and nothing you say will embarrass or disturb me."

Here she smiled again, and I detected a blush in her lovely pale skin. "I have no complaints at all in that area. It has always been wonderful and if anything has become better. I half suspect that the thrice-married Mrs. Ellen Terry, who is Esmeralda to his Quasimodo, has given him a lecture or two on how to better attend to the needs and desires of his wife, and he has taken the advice to heart."

"Yes, well, of course, she would know if anyone in London would. She is quite the adventurous and romantic woman," I conceded.

Here Holmes interrupted. "My dear Mrs. Neville, then why are we here? You have not given us a single hint of any reason. All the usual suspicions that lead wives to seek the services of a detective have had no play whatsoever in your life. What, pray tell, is the cause of your concern?"

There was more than a hint of annoyance in his voice. Mrs. St. Clair looked Holmes directly in the eye and replied.

"He can't act."

"Madam?"

"He is a brilliant scholar and an astute businessman, and he is totally incapable of doing anything requiring the least dramatic skill. At the Sunday School Christmas pageant, they gave him the role of Melchior, and he delivered his lines as if he were reading a report for the Foreign Office on the quarterly results for barley in Botswana. Even his son, who was playing one of the shepherds, told his father to put some more feeling into it. And all he could do was to speak the lines louder.

"Yet night after night, he is up there on the stage in front of hundreds of people delivering his words in a clear voice with just the exact amount of pathos, or anger, or pain, or joy or whatever emotion is called for. It does not make sense."

"It is unusual," said Holmes, "but not unknown for some men, or women for that matter, to be liberated in a way that your husband claims to be, and to experience an unleashing of their talents the moment the curtain opens."

She looked at Sherlock Holmes and spoke again. "And he can't dance."

"I'm sorry, madam. Dance?"

"He is a wonderful man, and I do not wish to disparage my husband in any way. But he is hopelessly clumsy. When he dances, he trips over his own feet and steps on mine. If he were to play cricket or football, he would be the most valuable asset of the opposing team. He is constantly bumping into the furniture, and if it were not for the banister to catch him, he would fall down the stairs once a week. Yet there he is on stage swinging from ropes by one hand, and holding a woman in the other. He scampers and leaps from the bell tower to the roof and back again in a manner that leaves the audiences gasping. He moves his body in one scene with distressing pathos, and in the next with dignity and energy. It is masterful to watch. And it cannot be explained."

"Are there some parts of your husband's past that he has never spoken of?" pressed Holmes. "Are there years or places that he will never reveal to you, or anyone?"

"I have searched my heart with the same question. He did some military service in the Cape. He did not enjoy it, and he never speaks about it, but up until now I had thought that it was only because he found it deadly boring, not because there could have been anything secretive, anything that could have had a profound effect on the hidden parts of his soul."

Holmes pondered a moment and asked, "Is there anything else?"

"The French."

"Mrs. Neville? The French?"

"As with many of the men who work in the Foreign Service at Whitehall, my husband had always spoken of the French with disparaging condescension. I have heard him say several times one could always count on the French when one wanted something to laugh about. Or that the entire history of French civilization was nothing more than *un folie de grandeur* writ large. He truly did not think very highly of them at all."

"And now, Madam," asked Sherlock Holmes. "How was your recent visit to Paris?"

She looked at him and then at me with a bit of the look that I had seen on so many faces of people when Sherlock Holmes has used his deductive powers of observation to deduce more about them than they thought possible.

Holmes smiled. "Your excellent shoes, Mrs. Neville, are far too stylish to have been purchased on any High Street in England. They are gleaming and new and could only have come from Paris."

She smiled back. "You are quite correct, sir. As you know, there are breaks from time to time in the performances of any long-running play. During the Christmas season, the Nativity spectacles take over, and there had been three other extended weekends when the theater offered some short new works. During all those times, Neville has insisted on taking me to Paris. He has become positively besotted with the city. He claims that he must be that way so he can become more a part of, in some sort of spiritual union with the character of Quasimodo. He said he had to spend time in the cathedral and the bell towers and the neighborhoods that Quasimodo spent his life in so that he could more faithfully portray him on the stage. When he first suggested this, I was tempted to say to him, 'Neville, darling, Quasimodo never lived in the bell tower. He never rang a single bell. He never, in fact, existed. Victor Hugo made him up. You might consider using your imagination just like Monsieur Hugo did.'

"But then I would have passed up a visit to Paris, so why object? After all, it is Paris. So yes, we have made four recent journeys there. We stay in the Hotel de Crillon by the square where the French chopped off each other's heads. He departs the hotel early in the morning to visit Notre Dame and the libraries and who knows what places in what *arrondissements*. He gives me a generous sum of money and tells me to enjoy my time, and I do. I have found several excellent galleries in Montmartre and have learned about the latest in French art. I have purchased a few of the paintings of their artists. My most recent was this one on the wall. It's something that one of their chaps, Monet was his name, did here on a visit to London. Do you like it?"

She pointed to a blurred oil painting that I concluded was supposed to be the Houses of Parliament at Westminster painted at sunset. I didn't have the heart to tell her that she had wasted her money.

"Does he meet with other people while he is there?" asked Holmes.

"He must, for he positively stinks of cheap French tobacco when he returns, but I have no idea as to who they might be, and he has not sought to introduce me, and that is all very well by me since the smell of them on his clothes is more than enough to tolerate. But the visits must be important as we are departing again on Maundy Thursday, and this time, we are to stay through until St. Thomas Day. After all, Paris in the springtime is not such a bad prospect, so I must not complain."

Holmes did not respond with a pleasantry. Instead, he took on a serious tone. "Has your husband given any indication that he might be in danger?"

Here the lady paused for some time before answering. "I had not seriously thought so until you asked that question, Mr. Holmes. Yet there have been some odd actions of his in the past three months, not in Paris, but here in Kent, which, now that you ask, lead to me to wonder."

"And what have those been?"

"As soon as he had begun his performances, he hired a man to watch our home in the evenings. He said that he would be away from six o'clock until after midnight for most evenings, and he did not want me to be unguarded. I thought it unnecessary, but I greatly appreciated his loving concern for me and for the children. Then he hired an additional man and extended the hours. Then he said that both of them had brothers who also needed work, and he was asked if he could possibly offer them service as well, which he did. I believe, sir, I am not entirely certain, but there may be as many as six men, all Lascars, and all quite fearsome chaps, who are prowling our grounds every hour of every day. Their pay is only a pittance, and they are very pleased with the steady work. They adore the children.

Some of them, I am sure, have children of their own in India and must miss them terribly. I cannot keep the chaps straight, but the children know them all by name and are not afraid of them in the least. They are awfully dedicated to our safety and could frighten away a mad dog just by looking at it. The number of them increased gradually over the past few months, and it did not occur to me before you asked that it had been because Neville was concerned for our safety. However, you may well be right, sir. I do not know."

Holmes said nothing more for a full minute. He sat back in his chair and gazed into the hearth. When he finally spoke, he said, "Madam, it is a terrible invasion of the privacy of yourself and your husband, but may I request your permission to spend the next hour carefully examining your rooms, and particularly the wardrobes, belongings, and office of your husband. I assure you that I will not disturb anything and that there will not be a trace of my inspection. I must also assure you that I would never make so inappropriate a request if I had not reached the same conclusion as you have and that there is something seriously amiss in your husband's life. Furthermore, I fear he may well be in danger. May I proceed?"

I watched as the color drained ever so slightly from the attractive face of Mrs. Neville St. Clair. She rose from her chair and quietly said, "Yes, Mr. Holmes. Certainly. Please follow me." She left the room with Sherlock Holmes following behind.

I sat in silence by myself for a minute until she returned. With a forced smile, she spoke to me. "Doctor Watson, I would not want you to lose your entire day because of your visit here. I am sure our groundskeeper has a fishing rod and some bait. You would be most welcome to try our pond, although it is not likely to be very rewarding."

I smiled warmly at her and replied, "It is perfectly all right, Mrs. Neville. I heard you say that your home has a good library, and if you would lead me to it, I would be as happy as a clam until my colleague has finished his inspection."

She did so most graciously, and for just over an hour, I caught up on several recent issues of *The Economist,* but could not decide whether I should be a Gladstone or a Disraeli in my response to them.

Holmes fetched me, and we paid our departing words to the lady of the house. Once out of the grounds and on the road back to London, I asked the obvious question.

"Well, Holmes," I said. "Speak up. Do you have any theories? What in the world is going on with this new-found thespian?"

"I have several theories, Watson. None of which has anywhere near enough data to support either its retention or dismissal. I do not expect to reach that point until Thursday, so kindly do not ask me again until then."

I shrugged, feeling as I often did a little hurt by his dismissal of me. Perhaps noticing my response, he added, "But we must stop in at the first telegraph office where you will send a wire to your good wife requesting her to be ready to be taken out to dinner this evening followed by attending the most talked-about performance in the West End. The three of us will meet in front of the Lyceum just before curtain time. I shall look after the tickets."

"Splendid idea, Holmes. And thank you for your consideration of Mary. But the play is sold out for weeks to come. There is no chance at this late date of getting any seats at all, let alone good ones. How can you possibly dream of doing so?"

"Elementary, my good doctor. A despicable trade has recently emerged in the theater district, and it is called ticket scalping. I fear that a few of my former Irregulars may have graduated into it. For a price that is well beyond criminal, you can always find decent seats for any performance. I shall send a wire off to Wiggins, the captain of my Irregulars, and I fully expect that he will find us three excellent seats adjoining each other. I will request somewhere in the front rows of the orchestra section. May I suggest Kettner's in Soho for your dinner. Their French cuisine is the best in London."

"Very well, Holmes. Any other suggestions?"

"Please change your clothes. Fishermen are not particularly welcomed in the theater."

Chapter Four

Quasimodo at the Lyceum

y dear wife, was thrilled with the prospect of an evening at the theater. I was concerned that she not be too disappointed if Sherlock Holmes's Irregulars did not come through with the tickets, and she graciously assured me that a dinner out in Soho followed by even an attempt at attending a play would be more than enough to please her. After donning a gentleman's evening dress, I hailed a cab, and off we went to Soho and dined on that quintessentially French delicacy with the quintessentially English name, Beef Wellington.

As time was not pressing and as it was a lovely spring evening, we walked all the way through Covent Garden and down to the Lyceum Theater. Standing in front of it, smoking a cigarette was the unmistakable figure of Sherlock Holmes. His smile told us that his scalping enterprise had been successful even if impoverishing. We entered and sat only five rows back from the stage; close enough to see the sweat on the actors' faces and the sprays of saliva bursting from their mouths as they delivered their lines.

When Mr. Neville St. Clair appeared, all made up as the hideous Quasimodo, there were audible gasps of horror from ladies throughout the audience, and some of the gentlemen compulsively looked away. His face was pale and disfigured by a horrible scar. A monstrous wart covered one eye, and the outer edge of his lip had been hideously turned up. For a moment, as a medical man who had seen more bodies mangled on the battlefield than could ever be portrayed on the stage, I felt anger at the way Victor Hugo had encouraged readers and audiences to treat physical imperfection with disgust, when what the deformed needed, and should have been expected in any civilized Christian country, was compassion. But then the magic of the theater took over, and I and the entire audience were drawn closer and closer to the character. Behind the ugly exterior, we could see the heroic, unselfish soul of a man who had a great heart. All of us were moved by his passion and devotion to Esmeralda. We cheered as our hero swooped down on the bell-rope and rescued her. Inwardly we all shouted to him, "No! No!" as he mistakenly fought off the Truands who are trying to rescue Esmeralda. More than one member of the audience involuntarily shouted out loud. Again we cheered when he became the instrument of divine justice and pushed the villain from the tower of the Cathedral. And, as Mrs. Neville had warned us, the whole house was moved to tears when this magnificent human being, confined to such an imperfect body, lay down and died beside the corpse of his murdered Esmeralda. Mary had tears streaming down her face. I shed a few myself, and I fancied that there might have even been a hint of one in the eye of Sherlock Holmes.

The entire audience leapt to its feet in thunderous applause as the curtain closed. All of the members of the cast were cheered on, but the greatest response was, as expected, for Neville St. Clair, as he shuffled, still made up and hunched over, to the front of the stage and took an awkward bow.

"Ah, that was magnificent, was it not?" I exulted when the three of us were on the pavement of Wellington Street. "Oh, yes. It was truly exceptional," echoed my wife. "Yes, indeed. Quite the unbelievable performance," said Holmes with a smile. Then he turned to the two of us and said, "Might I ask you two to join me for a few minutes longer, and wait with me and observe what takes place at the stage door?"

We agreed and walked to the back door of the theater from which the members of the cast would exit in the next fifteen to twenty minutes. There was already a small crowd of adoring fans standing there, hoping to have a close look at this new acting sensation, Neville St. Clair. Those closest to the door were mostly attractive young women, although there were two or three women of a certain age mixed in with them. Farther back on the sidewalk, there stood a group of gentlemen, the tolerant husbands, and fiancées of the ladies. They looked distinctly less enthusiastic and sullenly smoked, grumbled to each other, and affected the pained look that comes with indigestion.

Just a few yards up the street, I saw a handsome carriage, and in the window, discerned the face of the lovely Mrs. St. Clair. She caught my eye and gave a friendly wave and smile back to me.

A cheer went up from the group of women, and I saw Mr. Neville St. Clair come through the door and on to the pavement. He took a moment or two and chatted amiably with the women and then walked directly to the group of men. He had, I must admit, a commanding presence. Gone was the sickly brown tint to his face; gone the horrid scar and twisted lip. He was tall, broad-shouldered, and his military training showed in his bearing. One after the other, he shook the hands of the men and thanked them for their support of London's theater. The stage would not exist without them, he said as he humbly nodded to them. They all dropped their cigarettes, warmly shook his hand, and smiled back at him. As he walked towards his carriage, his wife stepped out, walked up to him, took his arm, and accompanied him until they were both back inside.

"Oh my," said Mary quietly. "He is very good at this, isn't he? The women are swooning, and the men all want to be like him. Well done, I must say."

"Ah yes," added Holmes. "Incredibly well done, yes." Then turning with a smile to my wife, he continued, "I thank you both for joining me at the theater. Mrs. Watson, I do not wish to deprive you of your wonderful husband more than is necessary, but I am in need of his support again on Tuesday evening."

"I am most certain that he would enjoy nothing more than another outing with Sherlock Holmes, so he is all yours, sir," she said with a warm smile.

"Even if I take him back to a smelly union hall?"

"It was I who sent him there the last time, so I guess it is only fair that it be your turn this time. You may do with him as you wish."

I interrupted with feigned indignation. "Pardon me, but as it is me that is being negotiated about, do I not get a say in the matter?"

My two best friends turned to me and in unison replied, "No." They laughed, and I had to as well.

The following two days were uneventful. Mary and I continued to talk about the splendid theater production and the stunning acting of Neville St. Clair. While I was attending to patients, Mary made an excursion to the nearest rag and bone shop and procured for me a worn but still serviceable working man's coat, trousers, shoes, and cap. After having them laundered, we agreed that they looked much more convincing for a visit to a union hall than my earlier attire.

As agreed, Holmes and I met on Salmon Lane, just north of the Limehouse Basin. He was once again in full disguise as an elderly cripple. I walked, and he hobbled to the Bar of Gold union hall. Instead of entering directly, he had us stand at the back of the hall and attempt to look inconspicuous while the would-be revolutionaries and saviors of France entered. Without my understanding why, he suddenly whispered "*maintenant*" and began to walk up the center aisle to a row just behind the front one. His ability to keep up his posture and disguise was a delight to watch. I knew that it must be dreadfully uncomfortable for him, a tall man, to walk hunched over at a near to sixty-degree angle, but it was yet another of his private disciplines that he had mastered in his pursuit of the criminal.

By seven o'clock, about fifty men of various ages had filled the hall, mostly dressed more or less like I was, except that I had not thought to add the French tam and scarf and by doing so had obviously not sufficiently announced my willingness to join the brotherhood, *le fraternité,* and those struggling across *la manche.*

The first speaker was a European chap with dark hair and a beard, named Herzl. He was introduced as a journalist who had been born in Hungary, worked for a Viennese newspaper, lived in Paris, and an expert on the Dreyfus Affair. I was highly impressed with his lucid, factual yet moving account of the terrible miscarriage of justice that had taken place in France. All of it, according to him, was based on nothing more than anti-Semitism. I found myself getting very angered and, had I been as young and impressionable as my nephew, I have no doubt I would have signed up for *le movement.* The speaker finished his talk to cheers and great applause, and I made a note in my mind to watch for this chap. He was destined to become quite important someday.

The second fellow to speak was an English fellow who spoke on behalf of his French cousin, Colonel Piquart, one of the leaders in the fight to defend Alfred Dreyfus. He was given a warm round of applause, mostly intended for his cousin, but nonetheless welcoming and appreciative. He ascended to the platform, stood behind the podium, grasped the lectern firmly with both hands, and began his talk.

He had not gotten more than a few words out when from the corner of my eye, I saw a figure lean through a window of the balcony, extend a gun, and begin shooting. The first and second shots appeared to hit the speaker, and he crumpled onto the floor. The gun was then turned towards the audience, and the killer began to shoot in our direction. Holmes dove to the floor, taking the stranger on his left with him. I followed suit and did the same, pulling the chap on my right down with me. There were panicked shouts everywhere. The killer's first shot hit and shattered the back of the chair to the left of Holmes but hit no one, thank God, and before he could fire off another, I heard the loud bang of a revolver fired from the back of the hall. The head of the killer in the window snapped back violently, and he fell out of sight.

General mayhem ensued. I saw Holmes move quickly until his mouth was against the ear of the man he had dragged to the floor. He must have said something, for the man looked at Holmes for a second in shock, and then leapt to his feet and ran quickly, pushing his way through the crowd until he got out the back door.

I stood and turned towards the stage with the intent of giving whatever medical assistance I could offer, but the strong hand of Sherlock Holmes grabbed onto the tail of my coat and held me back. "*Il est mort. Venez avec moi,*" he said, not giving up his disguise even in the thick of the chaos. With remarkable agility, he made his way, still bent over, through the crowd and out the door to the street. Only there, out of earshot of any others, did he return to his normal speaking voice.

"Up this stairway. He must have climbed up here to get to the window," he said. He bounded up the stairs, and I followed. To the surprise of both of us when we came upon the body of the shooter, minus a significant portion of his skull, a man was already bent over him and examining him closely with a magnifying glass. As soon as Holmes saw him, he immediately resumed his bent over disguise and staggered towards the little landing where the body lay.

The chap who had been looking at the body stood up, and I looked up into the face of an exceptionally tall man, several inches greater that Sherlock Holmes, who himself is over six feet. He was powerfully built and must have weighed in at over thirteen stone. There was a police inspector's badge attached to his coat, but I did not recognize him at all from our many colleagues at Scotland Yard. He gave Holmes and me a quick look over and then spoke, again surprising me with his American accent.

"I reckon I'm looking at Sherlock Holmes and John Watson, am I not? Golly, Mr. Holmes, why don't you just straighten up, it must get powerful uncomfortable keeping up that pose for as long as you have."

Holmes stared at this stranger with the type of perplexed look that I did not often see on the face of England's greatest detective. As he unbent his back, the stranger extended his hand, "Name's

Black. Ezekiel Black. Honored to meet you two. Y'all are part of my reason for being in England. Just didn't expect to be meeting you quite under these here circumstances."

Holmes shook the large, powerful hand rather tentatively, and I did the same. The American said, "I reckon you will want to take a close look at this fellow and all around him for clues, seeing as that's what I know you always do, sir. But I might save you a bit of working time by pointing out that there was nothing in his pockets at all, but there's a pile of cigarette ashes over there where he must have been waiting. You might want to look at them, but I reckon you'll find that they're *Gitaines.* You know, sir, the poor French version of *Gauloises.* I read your monograph on the one hundred and forty brands of tobacco, Mr. Holmes. Learned a powerful lot from that, sir. And his pistol, well it's a MAS 1873, but I reckon you knew that from the sound of it going off."

"And yours," said Holmes coolly, "must have been the Colt 45 fired from the back of the hall. Most likely long-barreled, hence the exceptional accuracy. Quite impressive, sir. But since we have not yet had the pleasure of meeting before, could you kindly enlighten me as to how a gunslinger from the Wild West happens to be assisting Scotland Yard, and how you came to be attending this meeting?"

"First question is easy, Mr. Holmes. I'm a US Marshal, and I asked for leave to come and see how you fellows do your stuff here with Scotland Yard. That's the official line. But the truth is I been reading all about you, sir, and I reckoned I could learn a thing or two from you, so I came over with the intent of meeting up. Got here just a week or so ago and those boys in Scotland Yard, well, they sent me on over here. Must have known you might show up I reckon. Said something about a message from some fella named Hayloft, or something like that, over in your guv'mint houses.

"Now if you two want to do some more looking just say so. Otherwise, I'll get this body to the morgue and report into the head sheriff down on the Embankment."

"Please proceed, Marshal," said Holmes with a level of sincere respect that he seldom exhibits for visiting Americans. "I am sure that we will have the pleasure of meeting again soon, or should I say 'see you 'round pardner.' " With this, he smiled. The tall American smiled back, and we turned and made our way down the stairs. Holmes did not bother bending over but kept walking upright until we came to a stand of cabs.

"If it is not too late an hour, my good man, please permit me to call upon you in about ninety minutes from now. I may have another proposal for your help."

He took a cab and drove towards the City, while I took one back to my house in Marylebone. At 9:30 pm that evening, my bell rang and, as expected, in came Sherlock Holmes. He took a seat in the parlor and, in a distracted manner, refused my wife's offer of tea. Brandy? That was accepted. Then he sat for what seemed a long time, sipping the brandy and saying nothing; discourteous if had it been from anyone else in the world.

Finally, I broke the silence. "Well then, my dear Holmes. It is not every day that someone shoots at us."

"Hmmm."

"That American sheriff was a bit of a surprise, was he not?"

"Hmmm."

"Oh, for goodness sakes Holmes, then here is one that you cannot answer with a 'hmmm.' What did you say to that bloke sitting beside you? The one you hauled down to the floor else he would have been shot. It looked as if you gave him a shock greater than the shooter had. He nearly jumped out of his skin and ran. What on earth did you say to him?"

Holmes shrugged. "I called him by his name and told him to get out of the place before the police detained him, and he had to identify himself as a witness."

"What? Well, then who was he?"

Holmes raised his head and, with a look of weary condescension, replied, "That was Neville St. Clair."

Chapter Five

To Paris

My wife let out a gasp of disbelief. I sat back in my chair. "Holmes. That's impossible. Neville St. Clair was on stage at the Lyceum all the time that we were in Limehouse."

"He was nothing of the sort and furthermore never has been."

This was too much for me. "Honestly, Homes, that is completely unbelievable. His wife delivers him to the theater. We watched him on stage for nearly three hours. We watched him exit from the theater. What do you mean he was not there? And how could that possibly have been him beside you? Holmes, that is madness."

Holmes took another sip on his brandy. "I do not know who that was on stage, although I have my suspicions. However, I am quite certain that it was not Neville St. Clair."

"Please, Holmes. How in heaven's name can you say that?"

"Oh very well, if you must. It goes like this. There were all the observations his wife stated, which could only be made sense of either by theorizing some secret previous life, the conclusion she had reached, or by the much simpler explanation that whoever it was onstage was not him. When I inspected his wardrobe, desk and belongings I noticed that the cuffs of the left sleeves of his shirts bore signs of wear and even some faint traces of ink, while the cuffs on the right were nearly new. Yet on stage, he clasped the bell-rope firmly in his right hand before he swung from the tower. He threw objects with his right hand, held off the Truands with a staff in his right hand, and pushed the villain off stage with the same. The tobacco in the ashtray in his bedroom at home was a fine bright-leaf Virginia blend. But when I visited his dressing room at the theater in the guise of a delivery service for the florist, I saw that the ashes were obviously of the Kentucky variety. And if that was not enough, it only took a good hard look at Neville St. Clair as he entered the union hall to know that he was the very same man we had seen exit the theater on the arm of his unsuspecting wife. He not only cannot act or dance, he is an amateur in the matter of disguise. And to top it all off, he responded when I addressed him by name and scampered away so that he could sneak back into his dressing room on time and not be delayed by the police."

"How can he possibly do all that?" I asked incredulously. "How does he escape from the theater dressing room and return unseen night after night?"

"That I do not know, but there must be a way since he quite obviously manages it."

I sat back in my chair, utterly amazed. "Very well then, Holmes. A toast. You have solved yet another mystery. His wife will be enlightened. The matter is resolved. Another successful case for Sherlock Holmes." I began to raise my glass when he cut back.

"That is idiotic nonsense, Watson. Enough. There was no mystery to be solved. Mycroft knew all along what was going on. He simply set me onto it to play yet another one of his games to prove he is smarter than I am. I have far better things to do with my time than trying to solve his riddles. It was not a case at all. It was an imbecilic waste of my time." With this, he drained his brandy, smacked the snifter down on the side table, and prepared to rise from his chair and leave.

My wife moved more quickly than he and seated herself in the chair immediately beside his and placed both of her hands firmly on his forearm. She leaned forward to look him directly in the face.

"Sherlock Holmes, you know perfectly well, if you would only use a little logic, that your brother Mycroft knows exactly how very clever you are and that he knew full well that you would see through Mr. St. Clair immediately, as you have. Obviously, that was the least of his concerns. The St. Clair family is in danger, and he has sent you to get them out of it. Even I can see that."

"Well then, he can jolly well just tell me what the danger is, from where and whom and why, and I can look after that. He doesn't have to play games!"

"Sherlock!" my wife shot back. "For pity's sake, if he knew that he would send in a few of his agents and have them do the job. He doesn't know the answers to those questions. Can you not see that?"

I nodded to myself and once again thanked the heavens for making me the luckiest man in the world to be blessed with such a wife.

Sherlock Holmes stared at her for a few seconds then slowly sat back in his chair and smiled. "I might enjoy another brandy, my dear lady, if it would not be asking too much?"

Mary rose and smiled back at him. "Fine, if you promise to quit pouting about your big brother, I will bring you a nice brandy." She leaned down and gave our difficult friend a kiss on the cheek.

She returned in a moment with a generous snifter. "There you go now. That will make things all feel better," she said with a loving laugh. "Now, you also told John that you had some other task in mind for him. What else is up your sleeve?"

For a full minute, he said nothing, obviously working through the next steps in his assignment. Then he replied. "Given your wise observations, my dear Mrs. Watson, I suppose that there must be a next task. It would concern not just your husband but you as well," Holmes replied.

"Yes?" said she.

"Is your calendar heavily booked this Thursday, Maundy Thursday, and through Easter Week?"

"Nothing that we could not move around a bit," my wife replied.

"Excellent," said Holmes. "The *Notre Dame* play is closed during that Easter period, and Mr. and Mrs. Neville St. Clair are leaving London for Paris for that entire time."

"And so what are we to do?" I asked. "Burglar their estate and solve more riddles?"

"Not at all," said Holmes. "We are going with them. You will have ten days in Paris, and I will send the bill to some miserable office in the bowels of Westminster. We depart first thing Thursday morning. I fully expect you to join me. After all, it is Paris."

The newspapers the following day were filled with screaming headlines about the incident in the union hall. One more murder in the East End was not worth mentioning, but in this case, the murderer had been identified as a Frenchman who had come to England and shot an Englishman. And that, of course, made it an international incident and worthy of outrage and demands that Westminster do something. Furthermore, the villain had some sort of ties to the French establishment, or the *Ancient Régime,* as Fleet Street insisted on calling it, conveniently ignoring the historical passing of said *régime* over a century ago. I read the reports in a cursory manner but was pre-occupied with hasty preparations for a visit to Paris.

Being an old campaigner, I could pack all I required in a Gladstone bag and be ready for an expedition in under an hour. Mary needed somewhat longer, as it was to be her first voyage to Paris. She was quite aflutter, choosing her wardrobe and pondering the endless romantic possibilities of a stay in the City of Light. By Wednesday evening, both of us were packed and ready, and early on the morning of Maundy Thursday, we made our way to Paddington in time for an early train to Dover.

On the pier for the ferry to Calais, I spotted the tall, thin figure of Sherlock Holmes, pacing back and forth and smoking one cigarette after another. He merely nodded at us as we approached and said, "I will meet with you in one hour on the top deck," and turned and walked away, lost in his ponderings. An hour later, we stood on the open top deck of the ferry and watched as the white cliffs of Dover receded into the distance, and the green hills of France emerged from the approaching horizon. Holmes had found himself a bench and was deep into what I imagined must have been his third pipe when we sat down beside him.

"My dear chap," I began. "I cannot object to a lovely excursion to Paris courtesy of Her Majesty's treasury, but I confess I am blind as a mole as to the reason."

Holmes said nothing, so I continued. "As England's best and only consulting detective, you are normally brought into a case by a client or by Scotland Yard to solve it when the crime that has been committed is too perplexing for those lacking imagination."

Again he said nothing, so again I continued. "Wherein is the crime that you have been called upon to solve? For the life of me, Holmes, I cannot fathom the reason for this excursion. A murder was committed at the union hall, but the killer was executed on the spot by that marshall on loan from America, so there is no unsolved crime there. Your client, Mrs. Neville St. Clair, was befuddled by her husband's antics, and you solved that problem in short order. What remains? What dastardly crime has been committed that requires your specialized services? Has something taken place in Paris? Is that why we are on our way there?"

Holmes slowly inhaled a long draught on his pipe and exhaled it in one long flume that disappeared into the morning breeze of the Channel. "It is not for a crime that has been committed that we are going there, but to prevent one, possibly a crime of monstrous and international proportions, that is about to take place."

"And just what might that be, pray tell?" I inquired.

Another slow draught was followed by another long and vanishing plume. "That, my dear Watson, is what I do not know. And that is what I must discover and then prevent from happening."

"I suppose," said I, "that it might be directly related to this Dreyfus mess. Do you truly believe that such a thing could be a threat to England?"

"Matters related to the Jewish people are always a concern to the British government," replied Holmes. "There is no end of popular beliefs regarding the Jews. There are some, such as that Herzl fellow we listened to, who want Britain to help protect the Jews who have returned to Palestine. There are others who claim that we who are Anglo-Saxons are descended from the ten lost tribes, and they are busy digging up a hill in Ireland looking for the Ark of the Covenant. And there are the Darbyites who are quite convinced that the return of the Jews to their ancestral home is a sure sign of the coming Millennium. All these beliefs are favorable towards the Jews. The last thing that Westminster wants is to have England torn apart if a popular movement of anti-Semitism were to spill over and sweep across the land as it has in France. So the Foreign Office is quietly but in a determined fashion doing everything it can to discredit those who have framed Captain Dreyfus, and to help his supporters."

"Am I to believe then," I queried, "that the meeting at the union hall was sanctioned and supported by Westminster?"

"Exactly. Else the speakers would never have been granted entry into the country, and the meeting would never have taken place."

"Who then was the killer?"

"Some poor fool sent by the anti-Dreyfusards, with the intent, I suspect, that the killing appear to have been carried out by an Englishman, and so send a message to the Dreyfusards that they would have no support from abroad."

"Ah, yes," I said. "Had the killer escaped, that would have been the story. But that all came to naught when he was shot on the spot."

"Precisely," said Holmes. "Had our Marshal Black, the gunslinger, not been so fast and accurate, the shooter might have escaped, and the press would no doubt announce that he must have been an English radical of some sort, an anti-Semite no doubt."

"Did Scotland Yard succeed in identifying the shooter? Was he connected to the General Staff? The Church? The *ancient régime*?"

"Yes, they did identify him. This letter was handed to me just before we boarded. Inspector Lestrade sent it with the note that it would give us some background information on the miserable assassin. I have not yet read it, so I propose that we retire to the galley for some tea and that you read it to me as we refresh ourselves."

Attempting to drink tea whilst sitting in the galley of an English ferry that is crossing the channel is one of the most hazardous activities engaged in by British travelers. Nevertheless, my wife and I managed to do so without making soggy messes of ourselves. I secured a teacup in one hand and the document Holmes had given me in the other and began reading. Holmes sat across from us with his eyes closed, his cup of tea cooling on the table.

"The Frenchie's name," I said, "according to Scotland Yard was Pierre Poutine, but there is a note attached that says this was a pseudonym. Believed to have been born and raised in the Jura since he speaks Arpitan as well as French, and may have spent some since across the border in Lausanne. Most recently, he was employed as a guard for some Marquis of somewhere I have never heard of. Did a few years of service in the French army. And there is a list of some private firms for whom he served as a payroll guard."

"Read the list please," said Holmes, without opening his eyes.

"Very well. *Saint Gobain, Le Procope, Suez, Lafarge, Investissements de Zurich, Société Générale, Crédit Lyonnais, Guerlain ...*"

"Stop there," Holmes interrupted me." Read again the fifth name." he opened his eyes and stared hard at me.

"Ahh, that would be Investissements de Zurich. Zurich Investments Limited," I said, providing a totally unnecessary translation.

I watched with growing concern as the countenance of my friend changed. The earlier look of peaceful reflection vanished and was replaced by one of cold determination. His eyes hardened, and I knew that something I had said had entirely altered the course of events in which we were engaged.

"What is it, Holmes? Who are those chaps? Can't say as I've ever heard of them."

"It is one of the most nefarious enterprises on the face of the earth. On the surface, they are a financial house with offices in Zurich and London. Beneath their respectable exterior, they are a network of criminals engaged in the most diabolical swindles, extortions, thefts, and murders. The name of the mastermind behind all of their operations never appears in any documents or on the lips of any of the employees. You have heard of him before from me. His name is James Moriarty."

"Is that not the devil of a professor you called 'the Napoleon of crime?'"

"Precisely. And now we know why Mycroft is sending us to Paris."

Chapter Six

A Radical Commune
Disguised as a Bookstore

T he port of Calais was busy and chaotic. It was the beginning of the Easter holiday for both English and French, and the traffic was terrific. The transfer from the ferry to the train should have taken no more than thirty minutes but took twice that long. Once ensconced in our cabin, however, we enjoyed the journey through Picardie and the north of France. The roses were in bloom in every courtyard, and the emerging lush spring crops of cereal grains, sugar beets, and potatoes stretched as far as the eye could see.

"Now, my dear Mr. Sherlock Holmes," said my wife as we approached the Gare du Nord. "Please enlighten us. Are Mr. and Mrs. Neville already in Paris?"

"They will arrive about two hours after we do."

"And are we staying at the same hotel?"

"No, my dear Mrs. Watson. That could put my investigation at risk. They are at their usual abode, the Hotel de Crillon. We are at the other end of the Jardin de Tuileries, at the Hotel du Louvre. However, tomorrow morning, immediately following breakfast, I would be most grateful if you would undertake to casually accost Mrs. St. Clair at her hotel lobby and accompany her for the day throughout the Latin Quarter, or the Marais, or wherever else she fancies visiting. That will leave your good husband and me free to pursue Mr. St. Clair."

"And does she know now of her husband's theatrical perfidy?" asked my wife.

"As of this moment, no, she does not," replied Holmes.

"And is she to learn of it? Is it not she who is your client?"

Holmes paused before answering. "I have vexed myself with the same question. My first obligation is always to my client. Yet if I were to inform her of my deductions, it would mean the immediate end to whatever it is that her husband is doing. The results of that action could be of much greater consequence. Until we are able to discern what is behind his most peculiar impersonation, we must leave Mrs. Neville in the dark and trust that she will not be unduly discomfited when the truth finally comes to light."

He said no more. From the train window, we watched the country carts, heavy with vegetables, making their way into the metropolis. The train entered the massive station, and we disembarked and, with the help of the Algerian porters, located our hotel's omnibus and made our way through the Tenth *arrondissement,* then the Second and finally to our hotel in the First, just a short walk to the Seine, the Louvre, and the pleasant gardens of the Tuileries.

Sherlock Holmes had visited Paris on several occasions and had done some very secretive detective work for the chaps at the Quay d'Orsay, as well as solving the Boulevard assassin case, for which the President of France had personally thanked him and appointed him to the Legion d'Honneur de France. He seemed quite familiar with the layout of the city and its sites and haunts. I had passed briefly through Paris during my days in the Army en route to the sub-continent, but it was my wife's first visit, and she was quite enjoying her encounters with the colorful cafes, shops, statuary, and wide boulevards of this most romantic of cities.

The hotel was one of the city's grandest. Indeed, Mr. Hugo Oberstein, a treasonous villain that Holmes had sent off to fifteen years in a British prison, had made it his European headquarters. I had to admit that the villain had had good taste. I noticed that Holmes, who normally eschewed sentimentality, was wearing his remarkably fine emerald tie-pin that "a certain gracious lady" had given him for acting in her interests in that matter.

"As our detective work will not begin until tomorrow morning," said Holmes while we stood in the magnificent hotel lobby, "may I invite the two of you to be my guests for dinner. The wonderful Tour d'Argent is only a twenty-minute walk from here, and it is quite famous for its *fois gras des Trios Empereurs,* and more ways of cooking a duck than can be imagined by anyone other than the French."

And so it was that an hour later we departed from the hotel, crossed the rue Rivoli and walked through the wonderful, stately courtyard of the Palais du Louvre.

We crossed the Seine at the Pont Neuf and strolled along the rive gauche for several blocks. Holmes, walking quickly as he always did, got out in front of Mary and me sufficiently far that the proprietors of the sidewalk bookstalls took him to be a single Englishman on his own in Paris and accosted him constantly with offers of racy and licentious postcards. He admitted defeat and slowed his pace so that he could walk alongside my wife and me.

We passed the impressive Place de St. Michel, where the archangel was doing in the devil. On our left, across the Seine, loomed the massive edifice, the Notre Dame Cathedral. It was a much greater sight to behold in real life than the small replica we had seen of it on the London stage just a few nights ago.

Mary looked up to the top of the south tower. "Oh my," she said. "That was the spot from which Quasimodo pushed the nasty villain. It must have been quite the terrifying site to watch him fall all that way." I would remind her at some later date that Mr. Hugo's story was pure fiction and simply did not happen, but for now, I would enjoy the imaginary story with her.

"It was, my dear," I replied. "And any minute now, we shall hear the bells ringing just as they did hundreds of years ago when the poor twisted man pulled tirelessly on the bell-rope."

We slowed our pace as we passed the long wall of the nave, looked up to the lovely high roseate windows at the top of the transept, and then at the ingenious architectural addition of the flying buttresses that kept the chancel from falling in. It was indeed quite humbling to ponder that Christian worship had taken place on this site for nearly one thousand years. Generations of French kings and queens had been crowned there, and of course, Napoleon had crowned himself, as might be expected.

Dinner in the Tour d'Argent was splendid. We were fortunate to have a table by a window and to be able to look down on the cathedral and the river as the gaslights, thousands of them, were lit one after the other, and the City of Light took on the romantic glow for which it is famous throughout the world. Following dinner, the three of us walked slowly along the banks of the Seine, enjoying the lovely spectacle that is Paris after dark.

"There are," said Holmes, "over 50,000 gas lamps in Paris. They light them all every evening. It does make it a rather pleasant place to live. As I have often said, you can always count on the French, at least to make Paris unforgettable.

"Tomorrow morning, however, we shall have to enter the demimonde of this lovely city. I shall meet you both at seven o'clock in the lobby. And now I bid you both good night, for it is now the hour when you, my dear friend, Watson, are accustomed to give your first yawn and look at the clock."

The following morning was Good Friday. I had feared that France, being a traditionally Catholic country, might have limited services available. However, it was springtime and a holiday, so all the wonderful sidewalk cafés were in full operation. We took our breakfast, feeling oh-so-very-Parisian, of croissants and strong coffee in an outdoor café in the Tuileries. Holmes had donned one of his favored disguises, that of a clergyman, and had adapted it to the continent by the addition of a *capello de romano,* which covered a rather shaggy set of silvery locks.

After breakfast, we made our way over to the Place de la Concorde, from where we had a commanding view of the entrance to the Hotel de Crillon from which Mr. and Mrs. Neville St. Clair were expected to emerge.

And so they did just after nine o'clock. They were a handsome couple and were clearly also overtaken by the romance of the setting, and also feeling oh-so-very-Parisian. They engaged in a long and passionate embrace and kiss before departing from each other. No proper English husband and wife, not even those in the theater, would have indulged in such scandalous behavior in public on the streets of London. But we were, after all, in Paris, and I could hear my dear wife beside me gasp, followed by distinctly heavy breathing, as she watched.

As agreed, my wife followed Mrs. St. Clair as she turned to her right and walked in the direction of the Champs d'Élysée. Holmes and I followed Mr. St. Clair as he walked quite purposely towards the Seine and the Pont de la Concorde. Having arrived at the far side of the bridge, he turned left and walked in the same direction as we had the previous evening. About a block past St. Michael's statue, he turned away from the river and crossed a small garden and entered a shop that appeared to be a café, a bookstore, and a rag-and-bone shop all put together. The sign above it read *Le Mistral, 37 rue de la Bûcherie.*

Mr. St. Clair entered the café and sat at a table just behind the window. We seated ourselves at another table on the pavement some small distance in front of him.

"Are you not concerned that he will recognize us?" I whispered to Holmes.

"The only other time he has encountered us, I was in the guise of a hunchback, and you were on your way to go fishing. So no, I do not suspect he will remember us at all, even if we were to speak directly to him."

The waiter first approached Mr. St. Clair and was obviously familiar with him. They both appeared to be speaking French.

"Holmes," I whispered. "I really don't know much French. Do you?"

47

"*Oui, mais pas necessaire, mon ami,*" he replied. "This is Paris, and you can count on all the waiters to speak acceptable English when they deign to do so."

The waiter, a gentleman of about fifty years of age and sporting a blue blazer, red cravat, and a black tam approached our table. He was not smiling. "*Quelques chose a boire?*"

"Good morning," said Holmes with a warm smile. "And would you, sir, be M. Marcel Schneider?"

The waiter looked startled and then glowered back at Homes. "That depends, m'sieur, on who it is that is asking."

"Merely a couple of Englishmen who have heard of the bravery of Captain Schneider during the war against the Prussians."

"Then you have not heard correctly," the man replied. But then he broke into a smile and added, "I was only ever a lieutenant, and I am very surprised that anyone from England would have heard of what I did during the war."

"Forgive me, my brave lieutenant," replied Holmes, again with a warm smile. "Permit me to introduce myself and my colleague. I am Father Dupont of the Church of England in Cambridge. My colleague here is Dr. John Paine, also of Cambridge, and a scholar of the French Revolution. You may have heard of his grandfather, Thomas Paine. He spent some time in France during his remarkable lifetime."

"*Incroyable,*" the waiter replied. "But of course, we know about Thomas Paine. He was a hero of both the Revolution in America as well as here in France. Gentlemen, *bienvenue à Le Mistral.* Allow me to bring you both some fine French coffee. None of that miserable, weak nonsense you serve in England. And for you, *mes amis, gratuit.*

"Good gracious, Holmes," I said. "How in heaven's name did you know all those things about a middle-aged waiter in Paris?"

"Elementary, my good doctor. His name was easy to come by if you listen to what the other waiters have been calling him. 'Schneider' is a very common name among the Jewish population of Alsace, as it borders with Germany. He has an obvious military bearing, as do you, my friend, and walks with a slight limp, no doubt left over from being wounded. His age is such that the only war in which he could have seen front line service was the Franco-Prussian conflict of some twenty years back. I awarded him with the rank of Captain, although I suspected that he might not have risen that far, but he would not object to being promoted. All really rather elementary, n'est pas?

Marcel returned to our table in a few minutes with two small cups of coffee, the consistency of which was sufficient to repair cracks in macadam. "M'sieurs, I know you are of the same spirit as the fraternité, and you are welcome here. Mais, I must caution you. The régime has spies everywhere. So please, gentlemen. Be careful."

"Are you concerned that they might send their spies here, to your bookstore?" asked Holmes.

"M'sieur, Le Mistral is truly a radical commune masquerading as a bookstore. It is the *siège social* of the Dreyfusard movement. But, of course, there are spies here." He bent over the table and lowered his voice. "If you look behind you, there is a man who has been here several times. He just sat down again. He is *un americain,* and a very strange one, bien sur. He pretends to be, *comment dit on, un garcon des vache,* a cow boy. He is plus étrange to be one of us." Marcel stood up and indicated with his eyes the direction of the latest suspect.

Holmes waited for a moment and then nonchalantly turned to look at the suspected spy. He turned back and struggled to muffle his laughter. I then glanced quickly as well. Behind us was a very tall man wearing a long leather coat, and what is known as a ten-gallon hat. On his feet were a set of finely tooled riding boots, such as might be found at a cobbler in Texas.

"Good heavens, Holmes. Isn't that . . . ? Isn't he . . .?

"Exactly. Our US marshal. He clearly has no desire to disguise his identity, but I am curious as to how he found himself and this place in Paris."

As if he had overhead, the marshal rose and strode over to our table, pulled up a chair, and seated himself.

"Mr. Holmes, Doctor Watson. Real nice to see you two hombres again. Real fine disguise you have there, Mr. Holmes. Can't say I would ever suspect you to be a parson. No point me doing a disguise. I'm afraid I'm too tall, and I never go anywhere without my boots or my side iron. Now I won't bother you two for too long, else these Frenchies will be thinking that you're spies like they think I am. So maybe the two of you should just look uppity for a minute, like as you are not real pleased by my talking to you. But I thought you might like to know that the English fellow that you followed here, well he's sitting at a table inside with two Frenchies and they're real deep into something. I'd like real bad to be listening in, but I could not pull off something like that. But you two could. If you look at the ceiling above their heads, you can see an open air vent to the next floor. I'm guessing that anyone who just put an ear to that vent could follow just about everything that's getting said. At least that's my suggestion, and you can take it for what it's worth, pardners."

He withdrew his long legs from under the table and made as if to depart.

"Just one more moment of your time, sir, if you will," said Holmes. "Mr. Black, I believe you said your name is, the last time we met."

"Well now, to be real formal, it's the Reverend Ezekiel Black. You can call me Zeke. That's what my pardners in the marshals call me."

"A man of the cloth?" said Holmes. "I would not have suspected."

"All goes back to the day when I had a revelation from the Almighty. I saw that I could either preach divine justice, or I could be an instrument for administering it. I chose the latter, and indeed, sir, I have been saving souls, and punishing a few, ever since."

"Very well then, Rev. Black," continued Holmes. "You appear to have some skills and imagination as a detective, and I look forward to our mutual cooperation. But, pray tell, just how do you expect Doctor Watson and me to enter this establishment, proceed to the next floor, and park ourselves beside an open grate in the floor

50

without being alarmingly conspicuous? I am intrigued by your suggestion, and I assume that you have an answer?"

"I been looking at this here place off and on over the past couple of days as part of what those boys at Scotland Yard have me doing for them. It's not just a bookstore and café. It's also a bit of what we in America might call a flophouse. There's about twenty radical types, young and old, who live on the upper floors, and they come tumbling down the stairs in the mornings, and then tumble back in here at night. Some stay for a night, some for days. Out in the West, we might call them "tumbleweeds" seeing as they ain't got no roots and just seem to blow in and back out again. But since Marcel thinks you two are part of the *fra-tour-nee-tay* I would be guessing that you could just mosey on inside and pretend you need some shut-eye for a hour or two, and do all the spying you need.

"Now I'll have to be getting up and leaving you two before they think that you're in cahoots with me and just another Yankee spy. Course I may be a lot of things, but I do object to being thought of as a Yankee, but this is Paris, and you can always count on the French to be a bit confused about some things. But that's my suggestion for you two fellows this morning. And I bid you a real good day. I have to go and have a talking to those Frenchie *gendarmes* about sending one of their hommes to kill another one of their hommes on English soil. So *ex-kyoo-say muah*."

With that, the Rev. Mr. Black stood up and walked away from the café and back towards the Place St. Michel.

After he had departed, Holmes looked at me and said, "For an American gunslinger, he shows a remarkable degree of intelligence and creativity. I suggest we follow his suggestion and see if we can observe our dear client's husband a little more closely."

He gestured for the waiter. "Marcel, mon capitaine. My friend and I are very fatigué from our travels. Would it be permissible for us to take some rest in the rooms above your café?"

"Bien sur. There are some blankets and pillows in the rooms. All friends of la révolution are welcome. *Faites comme chez vous.*"

We rose from the patio and made our way inside the café. I could see, as Rev. Black had said, that our lovely client's young husband was engaged in intense conversation at a table near the window. With him were two men, both considerably older, and all three had their pencils out and were making notes on pages of a document.

As we nonchalantly walked past them, I whispered to Holmes. "Any idea who those other two chaps are?"

"Yes," said Holmes, returning my whisper. "The one with the beard and the pince-nez is none other than the greatest living writer in France, Monsieur Émile Zola. The other one, with the walrus mustache and the balding head, is Dr. George Clemenceau, a hero of the French reformers, and now the highly influential owner of a very controversial newspaper. The entire establishment of France passionately fears and hates him. Our Mr. St. Clair has chosen himself some very interesting colleagues."

We made our way to the back of the café and up a steep, narrow staircase that I reasoned was long past the date when it should have been replaced. There were still a few sleeping bodies scattered around the halls and the floor. In the front room on the second floor, we found some blankets and pillows whose provenance I dared not contemplate. Feigning fatigue, we lay down on the floor with our heads on either side of the ventilation screen. The voices of those below us could be heard quite distinctly.

Propping ourselves up on an elbow, Holmes and I both scribbled furiously, recording parts of the conversation. Oddly, the three of them were speaking English and seemed to be working together on a translation of some manifesto that M. Zola had drafted. Dr. Clemenceau spoke English very fluently but with an odd accent that could have been mistaken for some American just off the boat from Boston. M. Zola, who I recalled had had a very successful visit to London some years earlier, spoke English with a distinguished Parisian cadence.

"What in heaven's name are they up to?" I asked Holmes when the trio below us had risen and departed.

Our pretended rest period having ended, we stood, and Holmes replied. "Monsieur Zola has written an extended accusation against the French government, courts, and military for their inexcusable actions related to the false evidence, conviction, and imprisonment of Captain Dreyfus. His friend, Dr. Clemenceau, is going to publish it in his newspaper, and our lovely client's brave young husband is translating it into English and arranging to have it circulated throughout the British Isles at the same time as it appears in Paris. He has been spending his evenings holding highly secret meetings with Dreyfusards living in England — British sympathizers and those who are leading the fight against anti-Semitism in England, which, I am sorry to say, is far more widespread than we would have wished. If his actions were known, he and his family would become the target both the anti-Dreyfusards and our own virulent haters of Jewish citizens. It is no wonder he has been so secretive about his affairs, even to the point of deceiving his devoted and adoring young wife."

"Do you suppose," I asked innocently, "that Mycroft is aware of all of this?"

Sherlock Holmes, from time to time, gave me a look that said, without speaking a word, that I was bordering on the edge between being a naïve dupe or a hopeless imbecile. I have been the recipient of such a look many times in my years of being associated with him. I had not grown to like receiving it any more in spite of the passing of time. Now I was once again the recipient of it, and knew immediately that my question was somewhat foolish.

"Good lord, Watson. Of course, he knows. I would not be surprised to find that Mr. St. Clair is reporting directly to his staff. No one can walk out on a posting to the Foreign Office on one week's notice, be granted an immediate pension, and land a plum role in the theater without someone in Westminster pulling strings."

I hesitated to ask another question but put on my brave face and spoke all the same. "How then could your Professor Moriarty be mixed up in this Dreyfus Affair? Which side is he on?"

Holmes refrained from his scornful look and gave me only a condescending smile. "Neither. That monster could not care a farthing if a French Jew was wrongly imprisoned or if one became the prime minister. He understands the ancient rule of ruthless business, that "in chaos there is profit." He is clearly intending to exploit this affair, and most likely working to intensify the actions of both sides."

"But how?"

"Again, my friend, that is what I do not yet know. I have several theories, but as of yet not sufficient data to form a working hypothesis. The incident at the union hall was his opening salvo. During our stay here in Paris, I shall have to discover all possible evidence of his next move. Otherwise, I have no doubt that Moriarty will inflict no end of peril upon countless people for the purpose not only of lining his pocket but for the mere joy he experiences in doing evil, triumphing over good, and profiting greatly from it."

Chapter Seven

Death at the Bourse

Holmes said no more while we walked along the Seine to the hotel. As we reached it I could hear the bells of Notre Dame striking the noon hour.

"I must leave you, my good friend," he said at the door of the hotel. "I have investigations to make which I can do better if I am not encumbered by your presence. I will join you and your good wife for late tea at five o'clock." With that, he departed, turned back the way we had come, and walked towards the Hotel de Ville. I shrugged, as it was far from the first time that I had been unceremoniously abandoned by Holmes. With an afternoon all alone in Paris, I treated myself to wandering through the Louvre for several hours.

It was my first visit to the great musée of Paris. For several hours I strolled wide-eyed through the magnificent corridors and great rooms ogling the works of art that I had read about since my childhood. I gazed at the ancient *Venus de Milo*, and imagined what her arms might have been doing had she not lost them. Likewise, I wondered what the expression might have been on the face of *Winged Victory* had her head still been attached. Though it was nothing more than a carved piece of lifeless rock, Michelangelo's *Dying Slave* was profoundly human, and the suffering and pain reached into my soul.

Then, of course, there were the enormous canvasses of David, who did his best to make Napoleon look heroic as he crossed the Alps. Likewise, Delacroix would have you believe that a bare-breasted woman holding a flag brought liberté to the people. The exquisite small paintings of the Dutch chaps, Vermeer, Rembrandt, Hals, Bruegel and Bosch, were all there to enjoy. Finally, I stood along with a small crowd of tourists, mostly Americans, and gazed, transfixed, at the *Mona Lisa*. She smiled back at me.

I returned to our hotel at five o'clock and found my lovely wife already seated and having tea with Holmes. She chatted amiably with the two of us about her day with Amelia St. Clair in the bohemian galleries of Montmartre, and then proposed that the three of us take in an evening spectacle at one of the somewhat risqué night clubs for which Paris is so infamously famous.

"With regret, I must decline," said Holmes. "My investigation of the events that have taken place, and are about to take place, has only just begun. I fear that I have come upon yet more violence perpetrated by the Moriarty syndicate, and I must acquire additional data. So, my dear friends, you shall have to enjoy gay Pair-ee sans moi."

"That is most unfortunate," I responded. "Pray tell, what have you come across?"

Holmes said nothing but reached for his portfolio case, opened it, and extracted a thick sheaf of documents. Out of this pile, he selected three sheets of folded newspaper and handed them to me. In a part of each sheet, I could see an article that he had designated by circling it with a thick pencil. The first sheet of newspaper was from *The Times*. The second was in French and from a Parisian daily, and the third from a German paper in Berlin. The English story described the suicide of a young stockbroker in The City. Scotland Yard reported that he had shot himself in the head, and his body had been discovered by his landlady yesterday. While the reporter bemoaned the loss of young life, the article concluded that the event was perhaps not as tragic as it might have been since the man was a bachelor and left no widow or fatherless children behind. I gave a quick summary of the article to my wife. Holmes nodded quietly.

As I have very little French and no German, I handed the other two sheets to Mary, who has rudimentary knowledge of both languages. "It is an account of the same event, is it not?" she asked, looking at Holmes. "I can make out that both of these stories likewise concern the suicide of a young stockbroker. Although it is odd that a newspaper in Paris and another one in Berlin would also carry the same story. I would not have thought that such an event would be news outside of London."

"You would not have thought correctly," said Holmes with a bit of a condescending smile. "The event in London was not covered by the French press, nor by the Germans. If you read the stories more closely, you will see that we are not looking at three accounts of the same event but unique accounts of three separate events. Three young men, all stockbrokers, all took their own lives by shooting themselves in the head, and all on the same day." He stopped and said nothing more, looking at the two of us in his habitual supercilious manner.

"Go on, then Holmes," I said impatiently. "You have obviously deduced that something is amiss in these accounts."

"As I have observed on many occasions in the past: when a tragic event takes place, it is happenstance. When the same event happens twice, it is coincidence. When it happens three times, it is a criminal conspiracy. When all three are so well disguised that they appear to Scotland Yard, and the Sûreté, and the Nationalpolizei to be suicides, then it is for certain that there is a diabolical criminal mind behind the deaths. I have already had cables back from Mycroft that confirmed what I suspected about the chap in The City."

"Yes. And what was that?" I asked.

"That the young man worked at a brokerage that managed the trades of Zurich Investments, and that he looked after that account."

"The syndicate that you believe Moriarty to be behind," I added.

"Yes. This evening I must attempt to make contact with someone at the Bourse and attempt to determine the responsibilities of the unlucky young French chap. Then tomorrow I shall depart for Berlin to do the same with regards to the German victim. So, my friends, I shall have to bid you adieu and even at this late hour find a registered trading agent of the Bourse who can assist me." He reached for his portfolio case and began to return the papers to it.

"No, Sherlock. You will do nothing of the sort," said my wife. He looked back at her immediately with a not entirely pleased looked on his face.

She smiled at him, reached into her purse, took out a calling card, and handed it to him.

"This lovely gentleman will, I am sure, be only too pleased to meet with you tomorrow and give you all the information you need."

Holmes, scowling, took the card and read it and then looked and smiled warmly at Mary as he read it aloud.

"Monsieur Charles Ephrussi. Banquier et Marchand d'Art. 11, avenue d'Iéna. And just how, permit me to ask, Mrs. Watson, did you come to be on such good terms with one of the wealthiest men in Paris?"

"Amelia St. Clair and I were visiting a fascinating small gallery in Montmartre, one of those with all those paintings that John keeps calling smudgy but which are all the most très avant guarde here in Paris. He began to chat with us, of course what French gentleman would not want to chat with two young unaccompanied Englishwomen, and he was not only impressed by our, well I should say Amelia's, interest in Parisian artists, but was positively thrilled when he learned that I was here in Paris with my husband, Dr. John Watson, the author of all those famous detective stories, and was absolutely over the moon when I told him that Sherlock Holmes, in the flesh, was in Paris. He is a most devoted fan of yours, Mr. Sherlock Holmes.

"And then I told him that you were doing some sort of investigating regarding the Dreyfus affair. I hope you did not mind my telling him that, but as he is a leading member of the Jewish community in Paris, I knew he would be interested, and probably very helpful. And he absolutely implored me, in a most charming and French fashion, of course, to arrange a meeting with you. He suggested lunch tomorrow at his club. Well, I promised to do my very best, but I warned him that you might not be interested since you could, at times, become intensely focused on a case and impervious to all social intercourse, let alone dining. He, very suavely, of course, acknowledged that he had read about your occasionally difficult character and understood the obstacles, but asked me only to do my best, and then, well, he is French, and this is Paris, so he bowed and kissed my hand and bid us au revoir.

"But I am sure that if you have the hotel deliver him a note, he would be very pleased to meet with you, and most likely give you all the information you need. So, Sherlock Holmes, you now have no excuse. We are off to the French theater for the evening."

Holmes, with a twinkle in his eye, lifted his head into an aloof pose, and replied, "Really, Mrs. Watson, I am disappointed that you did not land me a Rothschild. You only secured the second wealthiest banker in Paris; one who only controls six seats on the Bourse exchange."

And then he broke into a quiet laugh. "Well done, my dear lady. If you will excuse me for a few minutes, I will write a note to your charming and suave Monsieur Ephrussi, and then we shall be off to Place Pigalle for the raciest nightlife on the continent."

Half an hour later we climbed into a cab and traveled north along rue Montmartre through the second and ninth arrondissements and up the hill to Pigalle in the eighteenth. The open square was alive with a mix of people. There were Americans and English and visitors from all over the continent. Some men were in uniform, and these were being accosted constantly by the famous Parisian courtesans of the evening. The cafés had spilled out into the street and were raucous with loud talk and laughter. Holmes led us through the crowd to a brightly lit building on the far side of the square. On its top was a massive red windmill, the blades circling slowly in the night sky. Ladies and gentlemen in evening dress were entering it by the dozens.

"Bienvenue à Le Moulin Rouge," Holmes said to us with a broad smile. "This spectacle, this most controversial of nightclubs, has only recently opened its doors and already the good citizens of Paris are trying to shut it down. I rather suspect that they will not succeed."

We relaxed over dinner and Champagne and enjoyed the lively music provided by the large orchestra, the skits and farce numbers on stage, the dancers, and most of all, the finale. At least forty dancers, all linked with their arms on each other's shoulders, entered in a line from the wings, every one of them kicking their legs high into the air and bringing the audience to our feet cheering to the music of the *Can-Can*. Even Holmes was on his feet, clapping in time with the joyful music. The sensuous dancers kept kicking and dancing for several minutes and then took their bows to the cheers and applause of the enthusiastic participants in this highly risqué performance.

During the diner, I had watched an unnaturally short man a few tables away from us as he sketched with pastel chalk. He was doing charming drawings of the people at the various tables and then presenting his finished product to them for their purchase. Some tables bought his sketch, others shooed him away. When he came to our table, he presented himself to us as "Henri" and displayed a caricature sketch of the three of us. It was highly flattering to my wife, although much less so to Holmes or me. I was about to send him away when my wife reached for her purse, paid several francs more than I thought the thing was worth, and folded it carefully. I rolled my eyes at her extravagance and obvious waste of money.

We left the nightclub still in high spirits, and as it was a mild spring evening in Paris, we walked all the way back to the hotel, stopping along the way for a glass of absinthe. I do not remember a time before or since when I saw Sherlock Holmes so happy, as if he had not a care in the world. But by the time we reached the hotel, his countenance had changed. The smile had vanished.

"I bid you both, my dear, dear friends, good night. It was wonderful that we could eat, drink and be merry, for I fear that our time of joy has passed. Tomorrow the game will be afoot, and our gaite parisienne will be over. Please have a good night's sleep. À demain."

The following day Holmes and I met just before noon. The private club where we would meet Monsieur Ephrussi was undoubtedly restricted to men only, and so my wife had made plans to spend another pleasant day with our new-found friend, Mrs. Amelia St. Clair.

We walked the several blocks north, past the lovely gardens of the Palais Royale and towards the Bourse. The address we had been given turned out to be a finely tooled door with no nameplate on it. It was opened to our knock, and a butler greeted us by name and led us to a small private dining room. The wall and alcoves of the place were adorned with works of art, many of them priceless antiquities that I gathered Napoleon must have pirated from his time in Egypt along with the great obelisk that towers over Place de la Concorde.

There was not one but three immaculately dressed gentlemen waiting for us. They rose as we entered, and one of them, with a warm and genuine smile, walked towards us.

"Ah, Monsieur Sherlock Holmes and Le Docteur Watson, bienvenue à Paris. Our city is honored by the presence of the most popular writer in all of La France and by our favorite detective. Welcome, gentlemen, welcome." He spoke with a refined European accent and shook our hands warmly.

I was moved to reply. "Monsieur Ephrussi, the pleasure is all ours, but I cannot agree with your generous compliments. I am but a humble story-teller and cannot hold a candle to such a writer as your Émile Zola. He is an infinitely greater artist than I could ever hope to be."

"Ah, but of course, Doctor Watson. I did not say that you were a good writer, only the most popular. M'sieur Zola is a much better writer, but his books are long and depressing. So we do not admit to it, but the populace of France finds your stories to be plus agréable. And the hero of your stories," he continued turning to Holmes, "le détective manifique. Welcome, Monsieur Sherlock Holmes. It may have eluded even your practiced eye, but I am sure that as you entered these premises, you passed several financiers who were only pretending to read reports from the markets but were using them to cover the detective stories in which they were happily engrossed.

"And," he continued gesturing to the other two men, "permittez-moi to introduce my two cousins. Michel and Maurice Ephrussi. They are the true bankers in my family. They are the ones who earn our money, I am merely the black sheep who keeps spending it." The cousins smiled, chuckled, and nodded at what appeared to be an acknowledged fact of their family. "But please, we do extensive business with Threadneedle Street in London, so do call us by our familiar English names. This is Mike and Morris, et moi, je suis Charlie. And the services of the Ephrussi family and our bank are at your disposal, sir."

We shook the hands of Mike and Morris and seated ourselves. The white-gloved waiter filled our flutes with excellent Champagne, and we exchanged some pleasantries about the delight of being in Paris in the spring, the dreadful weather that plagues London, and our visit to the scandalous but exceedingly popular Moulin Rouge. As the Champagne was being poured for a second round, Michel Ephrussi, the senior of the two cousins, took over the lead in the conversation and turned it to matters at hand.

"Gentlemen," he said in an accent that varied between Ukrainian, French and German, "we are, as you must know, deeply concerned about L'affaire Dreyfus here in France. Our family and many of our colleagues in the financial world are juifs. We are Jews. This terrible affair has brought out from hiding some very antagonistic beliefs about our religion and our practices. We personally, and our bank, have been subjected to vile insults in the press and in the posters that unknown enemies continue to paste on the walls throughout the city. We are encouraged to know that the government of England is concerned about these events. Could you please enlighten us as to the actions your government has taken, and plans to take, not only in your country but to give support, in secret of course, to our brave Dreyfusards here in France?"

Sherlock Holmes responded, and as we devoured our lunch, he gave an extensive account of the clandestine policies and activities of Westminster. Most of it was news to me. Sanctuary, Holmes explained, was being given to any Dreyfusards whose lives were in danger. Currency exchange and transfer restrictions had been waived on funds sent across the Channel, and anti-Semitic leaders and their activities were being closely watched and frustrated with the type of petty interference and endless delays that only government bureaucrats can accomplish. "All of these activities are being managed," Holmes told them, "by an exceptional young officer in the Foreign Service Department, a Mr. Neville St. Clair."

"This young man," said Maurice Ephrussi, "he must be putting himself in great danger. The monsters of the régime are ruthless. He is sure to be on their list of enemies to be removed. They will kill him without hesitation. How is he managing all this?"

"He has created an exceptionally clever way of being able to meet in secret several evenings a week and on Saturday afternoons with Dreyfus sympathizers in London. He appears to have fooled almost everybody, including his wife. I fear, however, that there is a spy in the network somewhere and that in spite of his very careful precautions, his role has been discovered. Only a few days ago someone attempted to kill him at the same time as the cousin of Colonel Piquart was murdered."

This was news as well to me, as I had believed that the shot fired in our direction had been at random. Little did I know.

"Ah, oui, we heard of this incident," said Charlie. "It has caused some tension between our countries."

"That, I now suspect, was the intent," said Holmes, "and I expect that not only will Mr. St. Clair's life be in danger here in Paris, but that more incidents are planned with the devilish intention of causing a serious rift between the governments of our respective countries. And it is in this regard that I am in need of your assistance. May I ask if you were able to secure the information I requested concerning the young broker who is falsely believed to have committed suicide?"

"Oui, indeed, m'sieur," replied Michel Ephrussi. "The reports circulated amongst the members of the Bourse led us to believe that the unfortunate young man had taken his own life as the result of his disappointment and despair following the end of a passionate love affair. While such an event is considered tragic and sad, we, as relative newcomers to France ourselves, have come to understand that it is bound to the passionate core of French culture, to the soul of a true romantic Parisien. So no great heed was paid to this news. Your suggestion to us that it was not an acte de passion, But was, in truth, a murder, was most disturbing; not least because the young man, a Monsieur Serge Gavroche, was employed by one of our competitors in the Bourse, one that as a rule refuses to hire Jews. The temptation to engage in *sang-froid* was difficult to put aside. Nevertheless, we have extended our deep and sincere sympathies to his family and colleagues at his agency.

"And oui aussi, Monsieur Holmes, you were correct in your suspicion that the agency for which he worked had the account of Investissements de Zurich and had made and settled several large purchases of stock in their name in the recent past."

"And were you," asked Holmes, "able to determine the specific enterprises in which they acquired an equity position?"

"Such matters," replied M. Ephrussi, "are not supposed to be public knowledge here in Paris but, *oui monsieur,* we were able, through our very fine network of friends, to find out this information for you. Here is a list of the most recent transactions of *Investissements de Zurich.*" He reached into his suitcoat pocket and withdrew two sheets of paper. One he handed to Holmes and then turned to me. "We have *aussi* a copy for you as well, Monsieur Docteur."

I looked down the list. During the previous three months, there had been over twenty purchases of large blocks of common stock in half a dozen French firms. Some quick mental addition indicated that the value was well in excess of two million francs.

"I am not familiar," I said, "with all of these firms, but from what little knowledge I have and from their names, they appear to all be involved in the production of arms and armaments. Is that correct?"

"Oui, docteur, vous êtes correct, all of these firms are manufacturers of the implements of war. They supply the products to the Département de Défense. We looked at this list and found it very strange. France is at peace now with other nations. There is no hint of conflict anywhere. There has been peace with England since the vanquishing of Napoleon, and even with Germany, there has not been conflict for the past twenty years. The government is not buying more than a minimum of war goods. These firms are not highly profitable. The House of Ephrussi would never think of investing in them. It would be a waste of money."

"Is it possible," I asked, "that this firm in Zurich has received secret intelligence about a conflict that is about to erupt, and is taking advantage of that knowledge?"

"No, Watson," said Holmes sharply before any of the bankers had a chance to respond. "There is no secret intelligence. Bankers have as good or better sources of confidential information as any criminal syndicate. Something else must be afoot."

"Vraiment?" said Charles. "But what?"

"That sir, I do not yet know," replied Holmes. "The data you have given me has made several theories possible, but it is not yet sufficient to form a conclusion. We can, however, be sure that the young stockbroker was not murdered because of a foolish set of stock purchases. I will have to make inquiries with my sources in London, and I will also have to make a journey to Berlin. I will keep you informed as to any knowledge I may acquire. The only insight I can now give you is my suspicion that this dreadful Dreyfus affair is likely to be inflamed in the near future, and has the fearful potential of extending beyond the borders of France. And now I must thank you, gentlemen, for your time and your invaluable assistance."

We had not yet completed our dessert course, but Holmes rose from his chair and shook hands with the three Ephrussi's. He thanked them again for their assistance and appeared ready to dash out of the club.

"*Un moment, monsieur,*" said Charles. "One final piece of information and one request."

"Sir?" said Holmes.

"There will be this evening a meeting of another branch of the Dreyfusards, those who are working on the legal defense of Captain Dreyfus. It is taking place at Le Chat Noir. Are you familiar with this cabaret?"

"I am," said Holmes, "though I would never have expected it to be a location for a meeting of reformist lawyers. It is more usually patronized by musicians, artists and the like, is it not?"

"Absolument," said Charles. "That is why it is such an excellent place de rendezvous for lawyers. No one would ever expect to find them there."

"In which case, we shall disguise ourselves as lawyers and attend the meeting," said Holmes, with a friendly smile. "You also said that you had a request, which I assure you that if it is within my power to do so, I shall be honored to fulfill."

"Ah, je suis désolé, but our request is not within your power," replied Charles with the hint of an impish smile. "It is solely within the power of your colleague, Dr. Watson."

He turned to me and said, "Docteur, if you come to recording the story of Sherlock Holmes's investigation into these matters, might you be so kind as to include some mention of the Ephrussi family? Forgive our boyish desires, but we would be the only bankers in all of Europe to appear in one of your very popular stories. It would be a folie de grandeur on our part, but nonetheless, it would be a badge of honor within our very staid and boring world."

The other two Ephrussi gentlemen could not withhold their laughter and echoed Charles's request. I assured them that they would appear as excellent assistants to the famous detective, which indeed they were.

Chapter Eight

Quasimodo in Paris

would have continued to exchange pleasantries with them on the matter, but Holmes was tugging on the sleeve of my coat. We said our farewells and departed. Holmes did not exactly break into a run while exiting the club, but he was as close to it as could be tolerated.

"Please, Watson," he said sharply. "There is no time to waste. I must send off wires and make travel arrangements at once." We returned to the hotel at a forced march, whereupon Holmes left me in the lobby. "I will meet you here at seven o'clock this evening."

My dear wife had made arrangements to spend the evening at the Opéra with Mrs. St. Clair and come evening. Homes and I took a cab back up to Place Pigalle. This time, however, we entered a lively cabaret two blocks to the east. It was a much smaller venue than its grandiose neighbor, and, in place of a massive windmill, had only a poster of a rather imperious black cat. Through the fog of tobacco smoke, we made our way to the back of the building. As we had the look about us of lawyer,s we were directed to a small private room between the kitchen and the entrance to the delivery door in the back alley. It was encircled with chesterfields and daybed couches concerning whose normal use I decided it was best not to speculate.

A small number of chairs had been assembled in the center of the room, and Holmes sat in one of these. I followed and sat beside him.

"Is that not . . .?" I began to whisper with my finger pointing to the broad-shouldered young husband in front of us. Holmes nodded. "And is that not . . .?" I gestured towards the long set of legs and decorated riding boots extending from one of the couches. Again Holmes nodded.

I must confess that the next hour was a rather tedious affair for me. I have not very good French, and one speaker after another droned on, as lawyers are wont to do, about the arcane details of French law, courtroom procedures, and legal strategies. Most of it went entirely over my head, but Holmes sat upright and attentive, scribbling furiously. I nodded off several times but was brought wide awake when I hear a shout from someone in the front row. The door behind the lectern, the one that led out into the alleyway, had opened. Two men appeared in the doorway. The first one raised a pistol and pointed it directly at the front row. Holmes sprang from his chair as if he had been galvanized, hit the back of the chair in front of him with his shoulder and bounced Neville St. Clair forward and to the floor just before the bullet would have hit him in the chest. It very narrowly missed Holmes and lodged itself in the back of the chair in which he had been sitting. The second man in the doorway moved forward and, with an underhand throw, lobbed what was obviously a grenade into the center of the room. I dove to the floor and shouted a warning, without thinking that French lawyers might not understand panicked English. As I looked behind me, I saw the tall American marshal leap into the air and with his long arm grasp the live grenade whilst it was still not far from the ceiling. With the skill that Americans must develop from playing their confusing sport of baseball, he drilled the grenade right back at the chest of the man who had thrown it. It exploded with a deafening bang. Most of the explosive force was expended in the back alley of the building. There was no doubt that the two would-be assailants were killed instantly by their own grenade.

I was not a stranger to the battlefield and had been in the midst of exploding grenades and mortars several times in the past. I took several deep breaths to clear my head and moved to examine the men who had been sitting in the front row. Some of them had their hands to their eyes and ears, obviously in pain, but none were bleeding or in immediate peril. I felt the strong hand of Sherlock Holmes on my arm as he leaned forward to speak quietly into my ear.

"Are any of them in need of your services?" he asked.

I shook my head.

"Then," said Holmes, "let us depart." He motioned me towards the back door that was recently the means of attack of our assailants. The alley was strewn with garbage that had been dislodged by the explosion, and the charred bodies of the attackers were lying on the pavement, surrounded by several men who had quickly gathered to the scene. We walked hastily out onto Boulevard de Clichy and hailed a cab.

"Hotel de Crillon," ordered Holmes to the driver.

"Holmes," I said. "Did you not mean the Hotel de Louvre? The name you gave him is the hotel where the St. Clair's are staying, not ours."

"No, my friend," he replied. "It is time we had a quiet chat with Mr. Neville St. Clair. I have a responsibility to my client, his devoted wife, and her husband needs a bit of a talking-to."

He said no more but withdrew from his pocket a notepad, and pencil and began to write a note; a challenging task in a Paris taxicab whilst moving quickly over cobblestone roads. There were several pauses for traffic and pedestrians on Rue la Fayette and again on Boulevard des Italiens, and at each interval, Holmes took advantage of the stop to keep writing. By the time we reached the Place de la Concorde, he had completed the task and folded the note back into his pocket.

I paid the driver, and we entered the lobby of the hotel. Holmes walked directly to one of the writing desks in the front sitting room and withdrew the note, a package of Lucifers, a short stub of sealing wax, and a signet ring. He melted the wax and sealed the note.

"That should get his attention," he said. "Please observe into which mailbox the porter places this note."

Holmes handed the note to the desk porter, and I watched as he placed it into the mail slot, bearing room number 432.

"Come, Watson. Mr. St. Clair will be along shortly and the note will bring him immediately to his room, where we shall be waiting for him.

I knew not to ask Holmes how we were going gain access to the room. I assumed that in yet another pocket of his suit, he was carrying the small case of exquisite tools that are prized by both locksmiths and burglars. I had seen Holmes use these tools most recently when we gained entry to the home of Charles Augustus Milverton, and again this time, he had the lock picked and the door opened in a matter of seconds.

"I continue to be appalled by the abysmal lack of safety these hotels afford their guests," he said as we entered the suite of Mr. and Mrs. Neville St. Clair. I refrained from commenting that the guests were quite well-protected against all but the most expert of lock-pickers.

The sitting room of the suite was spacious and tastefully furnished with several occasional chairs and a chesterfield. Holmes moved one chair so that it was directly facing the entry door, and I did the same with another.

"We shan't have to wait long," said Holmes. "My note informed Mr. St. Clair that a document delivered to his room needed his immediate attention, and I used the seal of Mycroft's office. It can always be counted on to bring Her Majesty's servants on the double."

In the dark and in silence, we waited only another fifteen minutes before we heard the key in the door. The silhouette of a tall, broad-shouldered man appeared as the door opened. He immediately turned up the gas lamp on the right of the doorway.

"Good evening Mr. St. Clair," said Holmes in a loud voice.

The poor chap once again nearly jumped out of his skin. His eyes were wide in shock as he was getting ready, it appeared, to flee.

"I am Sherlock Holmes," said Holmes, again in a loud and authoritative manner. "And we are here for your protection. Please, Mr. St. Clair, be seated. This conversation will only take a few minutes."

St. Clair stared first and Holmes and then at me. A moment later, he recovered his composure, smiled and nodded his head in our direction. He sat on the chesterfield across from us, folded his arms across his chest and smiled.

"I must admit," he said. "I had not expected a visit from England's most famous detective. And you sir?" he said, looking directly at me. "Dr. Watson, I presume."

I nodded.

"The unexpected," he continued, "has become the rule for my life as of late, so I must get used to it. Very well, gentlemen, to what do I owe the honor of such a visit. I assure you that I have not been poaching game from the Bois de Boulogne, at least not yet." His voice was calm and charming. He smiled broadly but professionally as he spoke. I returned his smile. Holmes did not.

"It is my duty to inform you," said Holmes, quite sternly. "That although you have performed quite brilliantly on your mission, you are being foolish and careless by openly associating with the people you have been and attending their not-particularly-secret meetings."

"Oh, yes, you are quite correct," replied St. Clair, again with a forced smile. "All those theater chaps over here, and the Hugo scholars might come across as a bit of a rum lot, but I assure you that they are quite harmless and could not do any serious harm to my reputation."

"Please, Mr. St. Clair," said Holmes sharply. "You are not an actor. You are a spy for Her Majesty. And frankly, I do not enjoy tackling you and pushing you to the floor so that you do not end up dead, leaving your wife a widow and your children fatherless."

Neville St. Clair dropped his crossed arms and stared, speechless, at Sherlock Holmes for several seconds. He then smiled again and nodded.

"Ah, so that was you. Remind me to express my gratitude to the good folks in the Foreign Office for providing me with such an excellent personal bodyguard. I am in your debt sir, for your actions at *Le Chat Noir*."

"And," I interjected, "do not forget the union hall in Limehouse."

"Oh come, come, Dr. Watson, let us not take credit where it is not due. Terribly unsporting of you, sir. That was some elderly French cripple who I must say had a strong left arm."

Both Holmes and I gave the gentleman a look of unbridled disdain. It said more than enough for him to understand the unspoken message.

"Oh my," he said. "I really am in your debt. You truly are a master of disguises, Mr. Holmes. And you appear to be telling me that both of these incidents were specifically targeted as attacks on my life, are you not?"

"Indeed, we are Mr. St. Clair. You have performed your mission well so far, and Her Majesty's government will thank you for your efforts on behalf of the Dreyfusards, and for keeping the vile tide of anti-Semitism away from our shores. However, sir, I am warning you that your days of openly associating with leading Dreyfusards in Paris or London are over. There is a traitor somewhere in the corridors of Whitehall, and your identity has been discovered. Either you must master the art of disguise, or you must carry on your meetings in a totally clandestine manner, as you have every evening recently when you have been somewhere other than on stage at the Lyceum."

Yet again, Neville St. Clair looked intently at Sherlock Holmes. "I must thank you for your sage advice, sir. I had thought that my efforts had fooled everyone. Even my dear wife suspects nothing. You have shown me that I am putting not only my assignment at risk but my own life and the well-being of my family. I am yet again in your debt, and I assure you that I will give close heed to your sage advice. Thank you, Mr. Holmes, Dr. Watson."

The man was clearly shaken but very quick to recover his outward composure. Holmes rose to bid him good-night. "I wish you great success in fulfilling your mission. It is important not only for England but for the entire civilized world," he said. "Now, we must be on our way before your good wife returns from the Opera."

Neville St. Clair stood and shook his head in wonder. "I see that you even know the activities of my wife. And yes Mr. Holmes, by sheer good fortune she happened to meet another lovely English lady here in Paris, and the two of them are indeed attending the opera. They have become quite good friends, and are intent on impoverishing both me and the other lady's husband in the fine shops and galleries of this city."

Now it was my turn to surprise our good officer of the Foreign Service. "I thank you, sir, for the warning you have given me, as the lovely English lady who is accompanying your wife is my wife, and her meeting with yours is anything but happenstance."

The poor chap shrugged, held his arms out with his palms up and looked at us. "Ah, *mais oui,* as the French would say. But of course." He shook both of our hands warmly and bid us *bonsoir.*

Chapter Nine

Professor Moriarty and Captain Dreyfus

Upon reaching our hotel, Holmes thanked me again for accompanying him and almost being both shot and blown to pieces. He then added, "I will take my leave of you tomorrow morning. Inspector Lestrade has provided me with an introduction to a tall, stout French police officer, an Inspector Javert of the Sûreté. Lestrade assures me that the man has a long family history in the police, and even if lacking in any hint of compassion and mercy is of absolute integrity and would die before taking a centime from anyone attempting to pervert the course of justice. Then I must take myself first to London and then to Berlin to investigate the so-called suicides of these other two poor young stockbrokers. I hope that you are your wife will continue to enjoy Paris and that you, in your guise as Dr. John Paine, will be able to learn even more about the Dreyfus affair and inform me of all pertinent data upon my return."

He said no more and turned and retired to his room.

The next morning Holmes was gone. As requested, I spent much of my time during the ensuing few days attending various meetings of the Dreyfusards and learning more and more about this sordid affair. As an Englishman, I really should have been immune to being shocked by the bizarre activities of our neighbors across the Channel.

Yet I was deeply distressed by the revelations of the breadth and depth of virulent anti-Semitism that had been embraced by, it seemed, half of the population of the country. Absurd old accusations of God-killing and blood libel, which had long since vanished from respectable English society, were alive and well and spreading like a disease across the towns and villages of the country. Among the hundreds who had been involved in the bribes and misappropriations of the disastrous Panama scandal, two Jews had been named, and so the entire sorry mess was made to look as if it had been a plot by the small segment of the French population who adhered to the Jewish faith.

In the late fall of 1894, Captain Dreyfus, a Jew from Alsace, had been falsely accused of passing military secrets to the Germans. The following spring, in a secret trial that had become known to have been an extreme miscarriage of justice, he had been convicted and subsequently sentenced to prison on the infamous Devil's Island. Evidence had since been made public that pointed unequivocally to the guilt of another military officer, who had been summarily exonerated. Now a movement was underway, led by the sector of society who came to be known as *les intellectuals,* to have the entire case re-opened. Those who sided with the corrupt judiciary and military were fighting tooth and nail to shut down the opposition. Demonstrations were being held around the country both for and against the matter. The Dreyfusards were striving to have the miscarriage of justice redressed. Those opposed not only disagreed but shouted slogans, distributed pamphlets and newspapers, and plastered posters that were viciously anti-Semitic. There was not a soul in France who did not have an opinion of the affair, and the division between the two sides had torn the République asunder.

Holmes and I had observed Émile Zola and George Clemenceau assisting the work of the Dreyfusards. As I listened in on the subsequent meetings, I heard the names of many other courageous men and women who were fighting back the tide of injustice and anti-Semitism. Mathieu Dreyfus, the beleaguered Captain's older brother, the poet, Anatole France, and such leading lights as Bernard Lazare, Auguste Scheurer-Kestner, Joseph Reinarch and Henri Poincaré all lent their names and their talents to the fight. Col. Georges Piquart, the head of the French Army's Intelligence, had become convinced of the innocence of Alfred Dreyfus and was risking his career by taking a leading role in exposing the false evidence that had been fabricated against Dreyfus.

Monsieur Zola had already written several articles excoriating the French people for their treatment of French citizens of Jewish faith. Now he was at work on an open letter to the youth of France as well as the magnum opus, *J'accuse,* that would be published in the coming months and would turn the debate into a national war of opinion. I had the opportunity, indeed the honor, to chat personally with the great writer himself on one occasion and although he was very friendly to me when I was introduced as a distant relative of Thomas Paine, he burst into a beaming smile and kissed me on both cheeks when I confided to him that I was none other than Dr. John Watson, the writer of the adventures of Sherlock Holmes. The French publishing house, Hachette, had recently printed French translations of my stories, and many pirated versions had been in circulation from almost the day after they were published in English. Monsieur Zola assured me that he and all of the *les intellectuals* enjoyed my stories, and he was thrilled to know that Sherlock Holmes had become involved in even a small way in their struggle for truth and justice.

"And will Monsieur. Holmes be attending our great *manifestation,* our rally this Sunday afternoon in support of the Dreyfus cause?" he asked me. I did not have an answer for him but promised that I would be there and that I would do whatever I could to have Holmes attend as well.

Towards the end of the week, I noticed a chap in one of the meetings who was wearing clerical garb, a capello de romano, and sporting a bushy mustache. I gave a nod to Mr. Neville St. Clair and slipped him a note complimenting him on his disguise.

It was now late April in Paris. In the springtime, the city truly is a delight. Mary and I enjoyed wonderful mornings sitting at the tables on the sidewalks whilst sipping on fine French coffee and nibbling fresh croissants that would, even if it is trite to say so, melt in your mouth. During the daytime, she and Amelia St. Clair continued their visits to galleries, shops and museums. In the evening, the two of us wandered the streets of Paris until we came upon what looked to be an interesting restaurant. We were never disappointed. And one late afternoon, we walked along the Seine until we reach the famed Eiffel Tower. We entered the marvelous mechanical lift that took us much of the way up and then climbed the remaining stairs to the top. The view of Paris as the sun sets and the lights come on must be one of the romantic wonders of the modern world.

On Friday, 23 April 1897, we returned to our hotel after dinner to find Sherlock Holmes sitting in a corner of the parlor. His eyes were closed, and his fingertips pressed together: a pose he often assumed when in deepest concentration. I sat in a chair opposite him and waited for him to return from the intense interior of his exceptional mind.

"Ah, Watson," he said upon opening his eyes. "How good to see you."

"And you as well, my friend," said I. "And may I ask the object of your thinking?"

Without saying anything, he handed me a paper from the telegraph office. It ran:

WELCOME BACK TO PARIS MR. SHERLOCK HOLMES.

MY BEST WISHES FOR A GOOD TIME HERE ON QUASIMODO.

JM

"What on earth?" I blurted out. "Who in the world could possibly not only know about your travels but also that you are here watching St. Clair? I assume that is who is being referred to as 'Quasimodo.' This is uncanny."

"Not at all, Watson. The message is from Moriarty."

"Holmes, that is insane. Why would the man you are here to thwart reveal that he is already on to you? He is giving himself away."

"Ah, but that is part of his nature. It is not enough to pull off a heinous crime. His pride in his work cannot let him resist the temptation of taunting me. He has to dangle his actions in front of my face and prove that he can execute his devious plot right under my nose, thereby trouncing me when I will be helpless to stop him."

"What," I asked, "is this devil planning to do? He cannot make the Dreyfus incident any more of a conflict than it already is throughout France?"

"No," said Holmes. "But he can escalate it into an international incident and draw in other countries, particularly France's traditional enemies of England and Germany."

"But how?"

"I do not yet have a complete analysis," explained Holmes. "But some of the data I gathered in London and Berlin are pointing in a very specific direction. It began with the curious incidents of the three young stockbrokers who all appeared to commit suicide on the same day. I have been able to demonstrate to the authorities in all three countries that they were each the victims of a cleverly disguised murder. The pattern of stock purchases the unfortunate men in London and Berlin had recently managed was very similar to those that the good Ephrussi gentlemen discovered here at the Bourse. The firm of Zurich Investments has also taken major equity positions in armament production companies in England and Germany. In extended times of peace, such shares retain a modest and reasonable value. However, whenever a war takes place, the value of such shares leaps upwards. Then there is a fortune to be made."

"But Europe is at peace," I objected. "It is two decades now since the last fight between Germany and France and almost a century since one with England. Every country on the continent is more concerned with trade and building wealth than with fighting each other. There is no serious possibility at all of war. What is to be gained by buying stocks that will only jump in value if war is declared?"

"Again, you are quite correct," said Holmes patiently. "Or at least you would be if the markets always behaved rationally and logically. However, they do not. Our astute financiers do not require that a war be formally declared before rushing to buy stock in arms companies. All they need is a rumor of war. Our diabolically clever professor does not need a real war, only for one to be feared, and he will have made a fortune on his investments, all quite legally."

"What then is your professor going to do? And when?" I sputtered.

"I have some theories, but no conclusions yet," said Holmes. "He is taunting me with his message, and I assume that he is dangling a clue in front of me, and while I am seeing it, I cannot yet discern its meaning."

He said no more for several minutes. He looked intently at the telegram, then closed his eyes, and then repeated the process. Suddenly his eyes popped wide open.

"The telegram, Watson. Look at it." I did and shrugged.

"What am I supposed to see?"

"The words, Watson. What about them does not make sense?"

I looked again and read the message out loud. "Only the wrong preposition in the second line. He says, 'my best wishes for a good time here *on* Quasimodo.' It should read *with* Quasimodo since he is referring to Mr. St. Clair. But that is most likely the mistake of the telegraph operator, a Frenchman no doubt who mixed up his English prepositions. It is a common if careless mistake."

"No, Watson," Holmes rebuked me. "Moriarty does not make careless mistakes. Watson, it has been years since I have darkened the door of a church, but you are a good Catholic. In the Church calendar, what is the name of this coming Sunday?"

"It's the first Sunday after Easter," I replied. "It is St. Thomas Sunday."

"I believe it is more than that. Come, Watson. Where is the closest Catholic Church?"

I was truly befuddled by this sudden turn but responded. "Notre-Dame des Victoires is just up the street."

"Come then," he snapped as he rose and donned his coat. I did likewise, assured only that Sherlock Holmes was most unlikely to have had a religious epiphany.

We entered the old church. Having been built over two hundred years ago, it was dark and quiet. The walls were covered with tens of thousands of ex voto offerings left behind by pilgrims and those seeking healings and blessings. I was tempted to suggest to Holmes that he leave behind his magnifying glass as a token of thanks to the Virgin of her intercession but doubted he would appreciate either my humor or devotion.

In the dim light, Holmes turned to me. "Where would they keep the Missal?"

"There should be one in the pulpit," I said. "It may be already open to the mass to be said on this coming Sunday morning."

Holmes walked quickly towards the pulpit, and the bounded up the stairs. I followed him. Crowded into the pulpit, both of us bent our heads over the Missal to try to discern the words of the mass.

"There it is," said Holmes in a *sotto voce* exclamation. "Read it. The Introit."

I ran my finger down the page until I came to the Introit. "*Quasi modo geniti infants . . .*" I stopped. "Why, of course. In past centuries this coming Sunday was known as Quasimodo Sunday." Then I stared in disbelief at Holmes. "Honestly, Holmes, how could you have possibly known this tiny morsel of the history of the Church? You really are unbelievable."

He smiled smugly. "I confess my dear Brother Watson, that my knowledge of the Church calendar is almost entirely lacking. But as a boy, I read my father's copy of *The Hunchback of Notre Dame*. When I searched my memory, the scene came back to me. The deformed child was left on the steps of the church on the Sunday after Easter. The sisters abhorred him and would not even look upon his poor ugly body, but the compassionate priest took him in his arms and named him "Quasimodo" because he had been given to the Lord to care for on Quasimodo Sunday.

"Moriarty did not err in his prepositions," said Holmes. "He has told us that he will do something this Sunday, Quasimodo Sunday, just two days from now. He is telling us his plans, rubbing our noses in it, and laughing at us."

"Well then," I offered. "It might have something to do with the public meeting the Dreyfusards are holding on Sunday afternoon." The look on Holmes's face indicated that he had not yet heard of the event. It always pleased me when I could surprise him with some tidbit of news that he was not aware of. "They're holding it at the Pantheon. The entire leadership of the Dreyfusards will be there, and they expect several thousand of their supporters. It should be quite the spectacle."

Holmes looked intently at me and then nodded slowly. "Ah, yes. It should be indeed. It should indeed. And now a few more strands of data begin to make sense. Right, then. "Let us get out of this place before some angel expels us for being original sinners. I suggest dinner together with your lovely wife, but as of tomorrow morning, I fear I shall have to absent myself one more time and attempt to convince Inspector Javert that a most unlikely event is about to take place, and however improbable it is the only explanation for all the data I have uncovered. Come Watson, dinner . . . in Paris."

Chapter Ten

At the Pantheon

e saw nothing of Holmes the next day, but on the Sunday morning, there was a message requesting that we join him at one o'clock in the afternoon at a café that backed onto the Sorbonne on Rue Soufflot. He also noted that both Mr. and Mrs. Neville St. Clair had been invited to join us.

"Oh my," said my wife. "This could be very interesting, indeed. Do you suppose that Holmes will expose Mr. St. Clair's double life to his wife? I have observed that she has quite a strong spirit. She might not take things quietly."

"Hmm," I responded. "You are right. I have no idea what Holmes is up to but this could be very interesting indeed."

As we had plenteous time and as it was yet another perfect spring day in Paris, we walked via the stately Jardins de Luxembourg. There we paused and observed fathers and sons flying kites together or sailing little boats on the pond, and endless women, young and not-so-young all svelte and so stylishly dressed, as only the women of Paris are capable of doing.

From the gardens, it was only another two blocks to the Pantheon. As we approached it I could see that there were some barricades encircling the massive building and assumed that the police had determined to keep the Dreyfusard demonstrators from coming too close to the walls of the edifice.

At the café, Holmes was sitting alone, his old briar pipe between his lips. His eyes had a twinkle in them; he chucked on seeing us and seemed an altogether different man.

I noticed that at a table not far from him was the US marshal, quietly reading a dime novel. As on two previous occasions his presence had been accompanied by violence, I became immediately concerned. Holmes must have noticed my agitation and, standing as we approached, reassured me.

"Dr. and Mrs. Watson, how good to see you on a lovely afternoon in Paris. I assure you I promise you a safe and interesting time."

I was not entirely at ease but smiled back, and we seated ourselves. Only a minute after we had seated ourselves a French chap wearing a tam, a dark blue coat and a white silk scarf sat down at a table rather close to us. I thought he looked vaguely familiar, but I could not remember where I might have seen him. He also pulled a book from his pocket and began to read it.

The three of us chatted for several minutes, and then Mr. and Mrs. Neville St. Clair entered the café. Mrs. St. Clair was all smiles as she approached my wife and, as is the custom in Paris, gave her a friendly kiss on both cheeks. Mr. St. Clair nodded and smiled but did not look at all at ease and gave the sense of a man who would rather be anywhere else on earth.

"Darling," said Mrs. St. Clair to her husband. "This is my wonderful new friend Mrs. Watson. It was so fortunate that we happened to meet up with each other several days ago on the Champs d'Élysées. And this, "she said, turning to me, "must be her husband, Dr. Watson, one of the most successful authors in all of England. And," she said, smiling in the direction of Holmes, "have I the honor of meeting England's most famous detective, the true Sherlock Holmes?"

"The honor and pleasure is all mine, I assure you, madam," said Holmes, with a gentlemanly bow.

"Mr. Holmes and Dr. Watson," she continued, addressing her husband, "are in Paris doing some research related to crime in France, and we are so fortunate to be here at the same time and be able to spend the afternoon with them. Mr. Holmes, Dr. Watson, please meet my husband, Neville St. Clair, late of the Foreign Office and now one of the leading lights of the West End."

I extended my hand to St. Clair. "Ah, yes. Delighted to meet you, sir. We enjoyed your splendid performance in the Notre Dame play just last a few days ago. It was superb, would you not agree, Holmes?"

"Truly an unbelievable accomplishment," Holmes assented.

We further complimented Mr. St. Clair on his triumph on the stage and exchanged some additional pleasantries about Paris and how it compared so favorably to London. As we did so, I observed the marshal continuing to read his book, turning one page slowly after another. The French chap with the scarf, however, had not turned a single page. I gave Holmes a nod and said, "I don't know what is wrong with these French waiters, Holmes. I suggest we go inside and rouse one of them from his nap and demand some service at our table." I gestured towards the interior of the restaurant. Holmes nodded and rose and walked with me.

"Holmes," I said in a whisper. "That chap sitting behind you, the one with the scarf, is not reading at all. He is eavesdropping on everything that is being said."

"In which case, my dear doctor, I suggest that you try to speak distinctly and loudly so that he will not miss a word."

"Holmes, please, do not mock me. We have already encountered killers here in Paris. That man could be dangerous."

"No, my dear friend. I assure you, he is not. Now please let us return to our table and order some Champagne. Our napping waiter is on his way."

He turned and made his way back to our table. I followed, but not at all at ease.

As we continued to converse, I took notice of the crowds gathering in front of the Pantheon. Some men carried several cases to the top of the steps and made a makeshift dais for the expected speakers. By two o'clock, the crowd had grown to over a thousand. Within another fifteen minutes, it had doubled, and people continued to pour into the open pavement in front of the great temple to science, the arts, and enlightenment.

"What, pray tell, is happening?" asked Mrs. St. Clair, looking at the now very large crowd that was extending back towards where we were seated.

"Relax, my dear," said her husband. "It is just the French having yet another one of their demonstrations. This one is supposed to be calling all the radicals and reform-minded types to voice their opposition to the old guard. The French do enjoy doing things like this. It should be over soon." He spoke with practiced calmness, but I noticed that he kept looking in the direction of the crowd.

"Oh, of course," replied his wife. "How very French. Well, as you say, darling, we are in Paris, after all." She laughed briefly and continued chatting.

We stopped speaking as we heard a sharp increase in the volume of collective voices emerging from the crowd. I looked over and could see that all eyes had turned to the front of the Pantheon. Behind the pillars, the great central doors had swung open. Then the two smaller sets of doors to the right and left were opened. A man scampered to the top of the speaker's boxes and shouted to the crowd.

"Emparons-nous du Panthéon! Le Panthéon pour Dreyfus!"

The crowd took up the chant. "Le Panthéon pour Dreyfus! Le Panthéon pour Dreyfus!" they shouted in unison, and then they surged forward and began to climb the steps and enter the building.

I noticed a worried glance come over the face of Neville St. Clair. He shot a quick look at the chap in the scarf, who looked back at him. Both men did not seem happy with what we were observing.

Holmes ignored the commotion and continued chatting with Mrs. St. Clair and my wife. Within a few minutes, the crowd on the pavement had mostly vanished into the interior of building.

"Oh, how fortunate," said Mrs. St. Clair. "They have all gone inside. Now we shan't be disturbed."

Again I noticed a furtive glance exchanged between her husband and the chap with the scarf.

We had reached three o'clock in the afternoon, and I heard the bells of Notre Dame in the distance tolling the hour. Then a most peculiar thing happened. Instead of stopping after the third hour, the bells kept ringing. They rang through four and five and six and did not stop.

Holmes ceased talking, rose to his feet and looked directly at the building.

"Yes, Mr. Moriarty," he said. "Your signal, of course. Quasimodo ringing the bell. How appropriate."

We all looked at him, wondering what sort of nonsense he was talking.

We then shifted our gaze to the building. From out of the adjacent alleyways and doorways, some thirty men came running quickly towards all sides of the Pantheon. They leapt over the barricades and reached the walls. Those I could see were spaced out about ten yards apart, and I guessed that those on the far side were the same. Each one of them knelt down to the ground and looked as if they were lighting Lucifer matches. Then they rose and ran back, again leaping the barricades, but instead of escaping, they were each tackled by two or more large men who had billy clubs swinging and handcuffs at the ready. As all this was taking place, an explosion occurred against the building. Then another one could be heard from behind the back wall, and then a series of them. Flashes of flame were bursting around the perimeter of the temple. Paving stones and dirt were flying in all directions. Clouds of dark smoke were billowing from the place that the explosions had happened. I could hear screams of distress from people standing nearby.

We all stood and watched in horror. The man with the scarf came to the side of Mr. St. Clair and clutched his arm. I heard his anguished voice speaking in panic. "Oh my God, Neville. They are blowing up the Pantheon. All inside will die. The entire movement will be wiped out." St. Clair looked at the speaker with a look of terror on his face. I started to push my way past the others in an attempt to reach the site and provide whatever medical attention I could offer. I feared that the carnage would be worse than my worst day on the battlefield.

Holmes reached out his long arm and grabbed my coat, and held me back. "Watson, stop. No one has been hurt. No one."

I looked towards the building as the smoke cleared and could see that the building was still standing firm, with no apparent damage to it." The crowds had begun to stream out of the building, and it was clear that all were unharmed, although very confused and shouting and running off in all directions.

Holmes then spoke loudly to the group of us. "Please, my friends. There is no danger, and no one has been injured. Please be seated!"

We sat back in our chairs very apprehensively. The scarfed gentleman turned away from St. Clair with what I thought to be deliberate nonchalance. Holmes had remained standing and spoke to us.

"Excuse me for just a moment. My pride cannot resist the temptation."

He walked from the tables out into the open square and, in a very loud voice, shouted, "Mister Moriarty! Thank you for your lovely little display of fireworks! My best laugh in weeks!"

He returned to his chair at the table. "Forgive me," he said. "It was not necessary I know, and somewhat childish, but I simply could not resist."

Confusion painted the faces of all of us.

The marshal stood and moved to our table, bringing a chair with him. He sat down across from Holmes and spoke. "Well now, Mister Sherlock Holmes. I reckon you have some explaining to do. Just what in the sam hill was all that about?"

"That, my dear pardner, was the foiling of Moriarty's dastardly plan and the undoing of his network in France. All in a few short minutes before your eyes." Holmes had a look of satisfied smugness to him that I had observed before when he had thoroughly trounced his criminal opponent.

"Keep talking, Holmes. This one really takes the cake," said Reverend Black.

All our eyes were on Holmes, except for those of Mrs. St. Clair, who had a very angry look in her eyes and a hard gaze directed towards her husband.

"Most certainly," said Holmes. "First, let me fulfill my duties as a host and introduce you to my other guests. Mr. and Mrs. Watson, Mr. and Mrs. St. Clair, please meet the Reverend Mister Ezekiel Black, a US Marshal on loan to Scotland Yard, and the newest member of my esteemed Company of Baker Street Irregulars. Lest I forget, an excellent shot with a Colt 45 and a remarkable ability for the catching and throwing of grenades" I nodded towards Black. The others stared at him in confused silence.

"Right. Where was I?" said Holmes. "Oh, yes. The explosions you heard were all caused by dynamite that was manufactured in England and recently transported to France under the direction of the diabolical Professor Moriarty. He has purchased very large stakes in numerous armament companies and needed an international incident to create a rumor of war and drive up the value of his shares. What better than the mass murder of over a thousand Frenchmen with explosives that could be immediately traced to England? It so happened that the first large gathering was held by the Dreyfusards. Otherwise, he would have murdered a thousand anti-Dreyfusards had they decided to meet in an appropriate location yesterday. Fortunately, his explosives had only a tiny amount of the force needed to bring down a structure as solid as the Pantheon, so when they went off, no damage was done other than the dislodging of some paving stones, which can soon be replaced. Thirty of the criminals in his web of evil were instructed to light the fuses when they heard the sound of the bells, and the police officers, over two hundred of them, courtesy of Inspector Javert, were waiting to apprehend them. Moriarty's network in France is now on its way to prison. Those apprehended will most likely inform on the rest of their gang, and within a few days, they will all be under lock and key. Moriarty himself is most likely on his way back to either London or Zurich, no doubt with his blood boiling in anger at yours truly. A fact which I confess brings me no small degree of satisfaction. And that, my friends, is what has taken place here this afternoon."

"Whoa down there a minute, Sherlock," said Black. "Are you telling me that your brilliant evil professor was too dumb to know how much dynamite he needed to bring down a building? If you don't mind, I just won't bother believing that one."

Looking at Black, we all nodded our agreement with his statement, all that is except for Mrs. St. Clair, whose glare was still fixed on her husband.

"An astute insight, Reverend Black," returned Holmes. "Although it is not commonly known by the English populace, or even by Fleet Street, all manufacturers of explosives throughout Great Britain are required to send copies of any large orders to Whitehall for their review, and to flag any that may be coming from any purchaser other than a known and duly registered mining company or similar firm. The shipment to Moriarty had been spotted as soon as it appeared and tracked to its destination. Or at least that is what Mycroft has told me, so at least some version of that story has some truth to it. Last night, between one and two o'clock in the morning, six of Moriarty's men placed bundles of twenty sticks of dynamite in strategic locations around the foundations of the Pantheon, more than enough to bring it down and crush all those inside. But then between three and four o'clock in the morning Inspector Javert's men dug up every one of those caches, removing all but one stick. Enough to give a good bang, but far short of what was needed to do any damage. The police erected barricades as if they wanted to keep the Dreyfusards back from the building, but in fact to make sure that no citizens would be in danger from the small explosions and pavement stones."

"My goodness, Sherlock," my wife burst out. "But then you let it go ahead. Why did you not just have them arrested when they were planting the explosives in the first place? Someone could have been terribly hurt."

Before Holmes could reply, Reverend Black did so on his behalf. "Because, madam, that would have snagged only a few of the bad guys, and a much less serious charge to be laid. This way, he gets them all, and gets them charged with attempted murder, treason and whatever else they can throw at them. All the better if you want them to sing and inform on their fellow felons."

"Quite so," said Holmes. "Now may I propose a toast to the all of you for the role you have played, even if unawares, in decimating an evil network and helping to avert what could have been a serious conflict between two major European powers. Will you all please join me . . ." He began to lift his glass when Mrs. St. Clair cut him off.

"No, Mr. Holmes. I will not join in a toast." There was anger in her voice and on her face. "That cannot be the complete story. To start with, who is this man at the other table who rushed over to my husband when the explosions happened?" She turned first to her husband. "Neville, who is he?" she said, just short of shouting, while pointing at the man with the scarf. The fellow at the other table turned towards her and gave a Gallic shrug.

Her husband smiled and replied, "Darling, he just happened to be there, and I guess mine was the closest arm he could grab in the mayhem when we all thought we were witnessing a horror beyond belief. It is an entirely understandable thing to do, at least in Paris, is it not?"

"Neville St. Clair!" Now Mrs. St. Clair was shouting at her husband. "You're lying. I heard him speak to you. He spoke in English with a Cornwall accent, the same as yours. He knew your name. And you were both terrified that the "movement", whatever that is, had been destroyed. Now tell me what is going on and do not dare lie to me." The last few words were delivered in what can only be described as a loud scream.

Holmes stepped in. "Dear me, again I have failed as a host to make proper introductions. Please, everyone," he said, gesturing first to all of us and then pointing to the man at the table beside us. "Allow me to introduce Mr. Henry Irving, the finest actor currently treading the boards of the West End. And he is here together with his dear friend, Mr. Neville St. Clair, two of the finest spies in the service of Her Majesty; one of whom is doing a brilliant job of portraying Quasimodo at the Lyceum. Please, Mr. Irving, do join us rather than just listening in."

The fellow turned and looked at Holmes, with shock on his face. He then relaxed, shrugged again, and pulled his chair up to our table. He shook the hands of Holmes, Black and me and nodded towards the ladies. My wife smiled back, obviously pleased to have met such a star of the theater and enjoying the surprise of finding that he was alive and well and living for the moment in Paris.

Mrs. St. Clair did not smile back at him.

"It is obvious," said Holmes, directing his face first to St. Clair then to Irving, "that you two have known each other well for some time; years perhaps. Would one of you care to explain?"

Chapter Eleven

The True Hero of the West End

The two of them looked at each other, whereupon St. Clair gestured to Irving that the floor was his.

"Mr. Sherlock Holmes, Dr. and Mrs. Watson, Mrs. St. Clair and Rev. Black: I am indeed Henry Irving, and I am currently playing the role of Quasimodo on the stage of the Lyceum.

"I was raised in the village of Keinton Mandeville in Somerset but grew up under the care of my aunt in Cornwall, where Neville St. Clair was my neighbor. His family was one of the wealthier in the city, mine one of the poorest. As boys of the same age and living close to each other, we became friends, great friends. Both of us excelled at school, so much so that our headmaster, a retired Army Intelligence Officer who inculcated in us a passionate love of the British Empire, passed our names along to the Foreign Officer as having the potential to serve in Her Majesty's secret services. I did not attend college but entered the theater, and have been most fortunate to have had some success therein. Neville has had a stellar life first as a brilliant student at Cambridge, and now as one of the youngest senior analysts in the Foreign Office."

Although he was speaking quietly, his trained theatrical voice was clear on every syllable and a sensual experience to listen to. We all, except for Mrs. St. Clair, accompanied our listening with warm smiles.

Irving continued. "As dear friends and as fellow conspirators, we have kept in contact both with each other and with our director in the secret service. A decade ago, both of us became members of the Savage Club, and Freemasons in the Savage Lodge, a favorite haunt of bohemians, actors, artists and spies. As I have traveled to American and to the Continent, I have regularly sent intelligence reports back to Neville. Whilst in Paris two years ago, I became aware of this miserable affair concerning Captain Dreyfus and its potential not only to weaken Britain's ally, France, but its dreadful power to spread its contagion over throughout Europe. The Foreign Office confirmed my assessment and gave the matter highest priority.

"It was determined that all possible support should be given to Captain Dreyfus and the Dreyfusard movement, but it was imperative that Her Majesty's government could not possibly be seen to be meddling in the internal affairs of our ally. So over perhaps one or two too many brandies at the Club, Neville and I concocted our plan of having me disappear and him to take over my role, thus freeing me all day and him every evening to meet with the network of those supporting Dreyfus and fighting against the despicable hatred of the Jewish people.

"He would arrive at the theater through the front door and immediately exit again through the tradesmen's door so that he could carry on highly secret meetings with all the parties involved. I would enter from the back door, slip into Neville's dressing room, do my own make-up, a skill I have developed in my years in the theater, and then strut and fret my several hours on the stage, and return to the dressing room just as Neville returned from his meetings. As I am an actor and assumed to have bohemian tendencies, no one was overly worried about my temporary disappearance from public life.

"Other than the unexpected involvement of this Moriarty fellow who we, quite frankly, could not figure out at all, the entire enterprise has gone off surprisingly well. We fully expect that the miscarriage of justice will be corrected, that Captain Dreyfus will be fully exonerated, the real traitors punished, and nasty anti-Semitism, which is terribly rampant here in France, kept to a despised minimum in England. And that, ladies and gentlemen, is the end of our story."

We all, yet again for Mrs. St. Clair who eyes continued to blaze in anger, gave a quiet round of applause at the conclusion of Mr. Irving's recitation. He gave a small theatrical bow in response.

"My dear Henry," said Mr. St. Clair. "I fear you have forgotten an important detail concerning our relationship to each other."

"I might have indeed, Neville," responded Irving. "Why don't you enlighten them?"

"Henry has told you," said St. Clair, "that as boys, we became close friends. We were more than that. If you look at the two of us closely, you cannot help but see that we are similar in height and weight, hair and eye color, and the shape of our noses. We were often mistaken for brothers, which, in truth, was no mistake at all, as we are. I had a wonderful father, and Henry had none, the husband of his mother having died while he was a baby. It seems however that his mother and my father were more than just good neighbors. Mrs. Irving was my father's mistress, and we are sons of the same father. And so it is incumbent upon me to introduce my dearest wife to her brother-in-law, Mr. Henry Irving, currently the true hero of all of the West End."

He smiled a hopeful smile at his wife. She stood, her face red with rage, picked up her glass of Champagne, and threw its contents in her husband's face.

"You bastard!" she screamed, loudly enough to attract the attention of those seated at other tables and the waiter.

"Please, madam," said Irving. "In truth, that appellation belongs to me and not to your husband."

She looked at Irving and now shouted in his direction. "And you fraudulent monster you can bloody well . . ." here she added a most vulgar expression which I cannot put into print except to note that it demanded that he commit a sexual act which, as a medical man, I can assure you is anatomically impossible. She continued screaming at her husband.

"You have lied to me! You deceived me! I am your wife, the mother of your children!" The volume, if anything, increased with each phrase uttered. "How do you expect me to ever again share my bed with a man who has made a fool of me?!"

She continued in the same vein with several more threats, the jist of which was that she was very angry with her husband and announcing to the world that she was terminating the marriage without further notice.

The waiter approached our table whilst she was delivering her soliloquy. "Thees lady, m'sieur," he said into my ear. "She ees Eenglish but she is acting like an Italian. Should we be calling zee doctor?"

"I am a doctor, and she will be quite alright in just a moment," I whispered back. "But she does now need another glass of Champagne, if you would not mind."

"Of course, bien sur docteur. Immediatement."

To his credit, Sherlock Holmes waited until she paused for a breath and sharply interrupted her.

"Mrs. St. Clair! I am no authority on matters pertaining to marriage, and it is possible that your husband would have done better to have trusted his wife, but I do know something about the laws of England. Had your husband voluntarily disclosed to you the full nature of his clandestine work and current mission, he could have been charged with treason, his assets seized, and you and your children would look forward to a life of penury."

This silenced her outrage, and she gave a very hard look at Holmes, who rose from his chair and continued his lecture.

"I do not make it a habit to strongly rebuke my clients, but I must also counsel that you, having become privy to details concerning Her Majesty's secret service, could yourself be charged with treason should you ever disclose them to anyone.

"And furthermore, madam, it is a severe requirement of the Foreign Office that any man engaged in such dangerous matters as your husband must take all possible precautions to protect his wife and family, which your husband has done most faithfully.

"And furthermore, madam, as a result of your husband's brilliant performance on this mission I have it on unquestioned authority, that he is to receive a promotion and will be assigned the role of trade consul in New York City, a posting that is accompanied by a residence, a driver and a very generous entertainment allowance."

Mrs. St. Clair slowly sat back down in her chair, still looking at her husband, but the anger had gone from her eyes.

Her husband looked up at Homes and spoke. "Are you sure of that, Mr. Holmes? That is news to me. What in heaven's name will I be doing in New York?"

"You would be spying on the Americans," responded Holmes impatiently. "What do you think our trade consuls do over there?"

"Whoa, pardner," came the comment from Rev. Black. "We Americans and you Brits are supposed to be friends. What do you mean, spying on us?"

"Oh, please, Mr. Black," snapped Holmes. "We are military and political allies, but commercially we are virtually at war with each other. What do you think half those blokes at your Embassy in Mayfair do all but gather intelligence on English commerce?"

We all were without words for a few moments as we contemplated this obvious truth.

Neville St. Clair broke the silence and spoke quietly across the table to his wife. "Amelia, my darling, did I just hear Mr. Holmes refer to you and his "client?"

Holmes spoke. "You did indeed, sir."

"Am I to understand," Mr. St. Clair continued, with the traces of a smile appearing at the corners of his mouth, "that my loving wife hired England's most famous detective to spy on her husband."

Mrs. St. Clair looked in some other direction, gave a small shrug of her shoulders, and replied. "It is possible that something like that may have happened."

Her husband continued. "And am I to further understand that during this entire time in Paris that your meeting with Mrs. Watson was not happenstance but part of a plot behind your husband's back, to which I was entirely taken in and completely duped."

"It wasn't all that difficult," she said again with a shrug, but a bit of a coquettish smile. "For a spy, you really are a little gullible, darling."

Mr. St. Clair rose from his seat and moved until he stood behind his wife. "Mr. Sherlock Holmes," he said. "Kindly inform your highest authority in Westminster that I will happily accept the posting to New York, but only on the condition that my wife, Mrs. Amelia St. Clair, be designated my partner with an equivalent security designation."

He bent over, gently placed his hand on the back of the beautiful head of his wife, tipped it back, and slowly planted a kiss on her lips. Her hand reached up and grasped the back of his head and held it for what, by English standards, was a scandalously long time for a public display of affection. It mattered not to any of us. We were, after all, in Paris.

Epilogue

he Dreyfus affair did not conclude as quickly and as happily as we had hoped. The case was re-opened, and a new trial held, in which Captain Dreyfus, in what was an appalling sham of justice, was again convicted but then immediately pardoned. The actual traitor, a Major Esterhazy, was tried and, unbelievably, acquitted and allowed to flee the country. It was not until a decade later that the Supreme Court of France finally intervened and fully exonerated Captain Dreyfus and restored him to the rank of Brigadier-General, to which he would have normally been promoted had the appalling events of his affair not taken place.

Émile Zola wrote and George Clemenceau published a blistering summary of the affair under the title of *J'Accuse*. For his efforts, M. Zola was put on trial for criminal libel, stripped of his membership in the Legion d'Honneur and forced to flee to England. He eventually returned and was hailed as the courageous man of principle that he proved himself to be. He died not long afterward, and was buried in the Pantheon, under the words *AUX GRANDS HOMMES LA PATIRE RECONNAISSANTE,* his remains resting beside Victor Hugo, Jean-Jacques Rousseau and the other heroes of the enlightened French.

Rev. Mr. Black worked alongside Sherlock Holmes for several more months and then returned to America, where he immediately began to use the science of deduction to solve crimes. I am sure that we will all hear much more about him in the near future.

Mr. and Mrs. Neville St. Clair enjoyed a highly successful posting in Manhattan and subsequently in the consulates of other allies of Great Britain. I assume that he continued to furnish Whitehall with invaluable commercial intelligence. Mr. St. Clair was awarded with an ambassadorship to Canada and, to the dismay of his wife, posted to Ottawa. To her chagrin, her son learned to play hockey, and she became what the Canadians refer to as a "hockey mom" and could be seen, warmly bundled, in the benches beside the outdoor skating rinks cheering on her son and hurling epithets at the other team's players. More than once, she had to be restrained by her colleagues from throwing a cup of hot cocoa at a referee. Today Mr. St. Clair is a very senior diplomat and constantly in the Press. You would immediately recognize him had I used the true names of this wonderful couple in this story.

Mr. Henry Irving went on to a career, *optimis optimus,* on the world's stage, and as a theater impresario. He has recently received a knighthood from the Queen. For the sake of the Foreign Office, I can only hope that he is continuing to be one of the Empire's most effective spies.

Mr. Neville St. Clair, on the other hand, never returned to the stage, as he can neither act nor dance, and is still, to this day, according to his loving wife, hopelessly clumsy.

Dear Sherlockian Reader:

I first heard about the Dreyfus Affair in high school history class, but it was not until many years later that I came to understand just how divisive an event it was. It rocked all of France in the 1890s and the first decade of the twentieth century continues to be one of the sorriest and most sordid events in European history.

The references in this story to the false accusations, miscarriages of justice, anti-Semitism, and egregious imprisonment of innocent people are generally accurate. Countless books have been written on the affair, and Wikipedia has an excellent summary. To the best of my knowledge the government of Great Britain did not get involved in the Affair. But who knows?

On my very first visit to Paris decades ago, I paid a visit to the legendary bookstore, Shakespeare and Company. I have continued to patronize it ever since and was privileged to serve as one of the sponsors of its literary festival in June 2010. Those readers who also love this bookstore will recognize the tribute to it in this story as *Le Mistral,* the original name of the bookstore opened by George Whitman on *Rue de la Bûcherie.*

Émile Zola wrote and Georges Clemenceau published the polemical essay, *J'accuse,* in 1898, the year following the date of this story. Its effect on the Dreyfus Affair was significant, and the courageous Zola was for a brief time exiled to England. I read the essay (in English) while at university. Perhaps you did too,

The original Sherlock Holmes stories were printed as pirated versions in France soon after they began to appear in England. The publishing house, Hachette, officially translated and published them in 1896.

The Ephrussi family was one of the great banking dynasties of Vienna and Paris. Their fascinating story has recently been told in *The Hare with Amber Eyes,* by Edmund de Wall.

Le Chat Noire was in business in 1897, and still is. The famous nightclub, the Moulin Rouge, did not actually open its doors until

1899, but that's close enough. The Hotel de Crillon and Hotel de Louvre were there in 1897 and still are. The Pantheon is still standing.

Warm regards. Thank you for indulging me. I could not resist sending Sherlock to the city of light and love.

Craig

Did you enjoy this story? Are there ways it could have been improved? Please help the author and future readers of future New Sherlock Holmes Mysteries by posting a review on the site from which you purchased this book. Thanks, and happy sleuthing and deducing.

About the Author

In May of 2014 the Sherlock Holmes Society of Canada – better known as The Bootmakers (www.torontobootmakers.com) – announced a contest for a new Sherlock Holmes story. Although he had no experience writing fiction, the author submitted a short Sherlock Holmes mystery and was blessed to be declared one of the winners. Thus inspired, he has continued to write new Sherlock Holmes mysteries since. He has been writing these stories while living in Toronto, Tokyo, Buenos Aires, Bahrain, the Okanagan Valley, and Manhattan.

New Sherlock Holmes Mysteries
by Craig Stephen Copland

www.SherlockHolmesMystery.com

This is the first book in the series. Go to my website, start with this one and enjoy MORE SHERLOCK.

Studying Scarlet. Starlet O'Halloran, a fabulous mature woman, who reminds the reader of Scarlet O'Hara (but who, for copyright reasons cannot actually be her) has arrived in London looking for her long-lost husband, Brett (who resembles Rhett Butler, but who, for copyright reasons, cannot actually be him). She enlists the help of Sherlock Holmes. This is an unauthorized parody, inspired by Arthur Conan Doyle's *A Study in Scarlet* and Margaret Mitchell's *Gone with the Wind*.

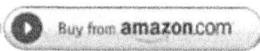

Six new Sherlock Holmes stories are always free to enjoy. If you have not already read them, go to this site, sign up, download and enjoy. www.SherlockHolmesMystery.com

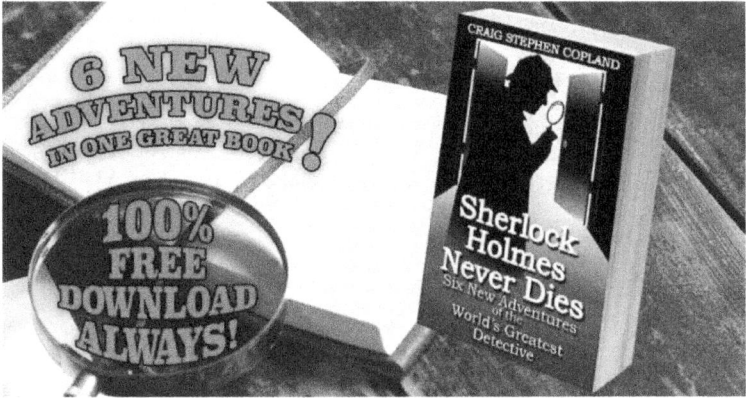

Super Collections A, B and C

57 New Sherlock Holmes Mysteries.

The perfect ebooks for readers who subscribe to Kindle Unlimited

Enter 'Craig Stephen Copland Sherlock Holmes Super Collection' into your Amazon search bar. Enjoy over 2 million words of **MORE SHERLOCK**.

www.SherlockHolmesMystery.com

The Man with the Twisted Lip

Twisted Lip

The Original Sherlock Holmes Story

Arthur Conan Doyle

The Man with the Twisted Lip

Isa Whitney, brother of the late Elias Whitney, D.D., Principal of the Theological College of St. George's, was much addicted to opium. The habit grew upon him, as I understand, from some foolish freak when he was at college; for having read De Quincey's description of his dreams and sensations, he had drenched his tobacco with laudanum in an attempt to produce the same effects. He found, as so many more have done, that the practice is easier to attain than to get rid of, and for many years he continued to be a slave to the drug, an object of mingled horror and pity to his friends and relatives. I can see him now, with yellow, pasty face, drooping lids, and pin-point pupils, all huddled in a chair, the wreck and ruin of a noble man.

One night — it was in June, '89 — there came a ring to my bell, about the hour when a man gives his first yawn and glances at the clock. I sat up in my chair, and my wife laid her needle-work down in her lap and made a little face of disappointment.

"A patient!" said she. "You'll have to go out."

I groaned, for I was newly come back from a weary day.

We heard the door open, a few hurried words, and then quick steps upon the linoleum. Our own door flew open, and a lady, clad in some dark-colored stuff, with a black veil, entered the room.

"You will excuse my calling so late," she began, and then, suddenly losing her self-control, she ran forward, threw her arms about my wife's neck, and sobbed upon her shoulder. "Oh, I'm in such trouble!" she cried; "I do so want a little help."

"Why," said my wife, pulling up her veil, "it is Kate Whitney. How you startled me, Kate! I had not an idea who you were when you came in."

"I didn't know what to do, so I came straight to you." That was always the way. Folk who were in grief came to my wife like birds to a light-house.

"It was very sweet of you to come. Now, you must have some wine and water, and sit here comfortably and tell us all about it. Or should you rather that I sent James off to bed?"

"Oh, no, no! I want the doctor's advice and help, too. It's about Isa. He has not been home for two days. I am so frightened about him!"

It was not the first time that she had spoken to us of her husband's trouble, to me as a doctor, to my wife as an old friend and school companion. We soothed and comforted her by such words as we could find. Did she know where her husband was? Was it possible that we could bring him back to her?

It seems that it was. She had the surest information that of late he had, when the fit was on him, made use of an opium den in the farthest east of the City. Hitherto his orgies had always been confined to one day, and he had come back, twitching and shattered, in the evening. But now the spell had been upon him eight-and-forty hours, and he lay there, doubtless among the dregs of the docks, breathing in the poison or sleeping off the effects. There he was to be found, she was sure of it, at the Bar of Gold, in Upper Swandam Lane. But what was she to do? How could she, a young and timid woman, make her way into such a place and pluck her husband out from among the ruffians who surrounded him?

There was the case, and of course there was but one way out of it. Might I not escort her to this place? And then, as a second thought, why should she come at all? I was Isa Whitney's medical adviser, and as such I had influence over him. I could manage it better if I were alone. I promised her on my word that I would send him home in a cab within two hours if he were indeed at the address which she had given me. And so in ten minutes I had left my armchair and cheery sitting-room behind me, and was speeding eastward in a hansom on a strange errand, as it seemed to me at the time, though the future only could show how strange it was to be.

But there was no great difficulty in the first stage of my adventure. Upper Swandam Lane is a vile alley lurking behind the high wharves which line the north side of the river to the east of London Bridge. Between a slop-shop and a gin-shop, approached by a steep flight of steps leading down to a black gap like the mouth of a cave, I found the den of which I was in search. Ordering my cab to wait, I passed down the steps, worn hollow in the center by the ceaseless tread of drunken feet; and by the light of a flickering oil-lamp above the door I found the latch and made my way into a long, low room, thick and heavy with the brown opium smoke, and terraced with wooden berths, like the forecastle of an emigrant ship.

Through the gloom one could dimly catch a glimpse of bodies lying in strange fantastic poses, bowed shoulders, bent knees, heads thrown back, and chins pointing upward, with here and there a dark, lack-lustre eye turned upon the newcomer. Out of the black shadows there glimmered little red circles of light, now bright, now faint, as the burning poison waxed or waned in the bowls of the metal pipes. The most lay silent, but some muttered to themselves, and others talked together in a strange, low, monotonous voice, their conversation coming in gushes, and then suddenly tailing off into silence, each mumbling out his own thoughts and paying little heed to the words of his neighbor. At the farther end was a small brazier of burning charcoal, beside which on a three-legged wooden stool there sat a tall, thin old man, with his jaw resting upon his two fists, and his elbows upon his knees, staring into the fire.

As I entered, a sallow Malay attendant had hurried up with a pipe for me and a supply of the drug, beckoning me to an empty berth.

"Thank you. I have not come to stay," said I. "There is a friend of mine here, Mr. Isa Whitney, and I wish to speak with him."

There was a movement and an exclamation from my right, and peering through the gloom I saw Whitney, pale, haggard, and unkempt, staring out at me.

"My God! It's Watson," said he. He was in a pitiable state of reaction, with every nerve in a twitter. "I say, Watson, what o'clock is it?"

"Nearly eleven."

"Of what day?"

"Of Friday, June 19th."

"Good heavens! I thought it was Wednesday. It is Wednesday. What d'you want to frighten the chap for?" He sank his face onto his arms and began to sob in a high treble key.

"I tell you that it is Friday, man. Your wife has been waiting this two days for you. You should be ashamed of yourself!"

"So I am. But you've got mixed, Watson, for I have only been here a few hours, three pipes, four pipes — I forget how many. But I'll go home with you. I wouldn't frighten Kate — poor little Kate. Give me your hand! Have you a cab?"

"Yes, I have one waiting."

"Then I shall go in it. But I must owe something. Find what I owe, Watson. I am all off color. I can do nothing for myself."

I walked down the narrow passage between the double row of sleepers, holding my breath to keep out the vile, stupefying fumes of the drug, and looking about for the manager. As I passed the tall man who sat by the brazier I felt a sudden pluck at my skirt, and a low voice whispered, "Walk past me, and then look back at me." The words fell quite distinctly upon my ear. I glanced down. They could only have come from the old man at my side, and yet he sat now as absorbed as ever, very thin, very wrinkled, bent with age, an opium pipe dangling down from between his knees, as though it had dropped in sheer lassitude from his fingers. I took two steps forward and looked back. It took all my self-control to prevent me from breaking out into a cry of astonishment. He had turned his back so that none could see him but I. His form had filled out, his wrinkles were gone, the dull eyes had regained their fire, and there, sitting by the fire and grinning at my surprise, was none other than Sherlock Holmes. He made a slight motion to me to approach him, and instantly, as he turned his face half round to the company once more, subsided into a doddering, loose-lipped senility.

"Holmes!" I whispered, "what on earth are you doing in this den?"

"As low as you can," he answered; "I have excellent ears. If you would have the great kindness to get rid of that sottish friend of yours I should be exceedingly glad to have a little talk with you."

"I have a cab outside."

"Then pray send him home in it. You may safely trust him, for he appears to be too limp to get into any mischief. I should recommend you also to send a note by the cabman to your wife to say that you have thrown in your lot with me. If you will wait outside, I shall be with you in five minutes."

It was difficult to refuse any of Sherlock Holmes's requests, for they were always so exceedingly definite, and put forward with such a quiet air of mastery. I felt, however, that when Whitney was once confined in the cab my mission was practically accomplished; and for the rest, I could not wish anything better than to be associated with my friend in one of those singular adventures which were the normal condition of his existence. In a few minutes I had written my note, paid Whitney's bill, led him out to the cab, and seen him driven through the darkness. In a very short time a decrepit figure had emerged from the opium den, and I was walking down the street with Sherlock Holmes. For two streets he shuffled along with a bent back and an uncertain foot. Then, glancing quickly round, he straightened himself out and burst into a hearty fit of laughter.

"I suppose, Watson," said he, "that you imagine that I have added opium-smoking to cocaine injections, and all the other little weaknesses on which you have favored me with your medical views."

"I was certainly surprised to find you there."

"But not more so than I to find you."

"I came to find a friend."

"And I to find an enemy."

"An enemy?"

"Yes; one of my natural enemies, or, shall I say, my natural prey. Briefly, Watson, I am in the midst of a very remarkable inquiry, and I have hoped to find a clew in the incoherent ramblings of these sots, as I have done before now. Had I been recognized in that den my life would not have been worth an hour's purchase; for I have used it before now for my own purposes, and the rascally Lascar who runs it has sworn to have vengeance upon me. There is a trap-door at the back of that building, near the corner of Paul's Wharf, which could tell some strange tales of what has passed through it upon the moonless nights."

"What! You do not mean bodies?"

"Ay, bodies, Watson. We should be rich men if we had 1000 pounds for every poor devil who has been done to death in that den. It is the vilest murder-trap on the whole riverside, and I fear that Neville St. Clair has entered it never to leave it more. But our trap should be here." He put his two forefingers between his teeth and whistled shrilly — a signal which was answered by a similar whistle from the distance, followed shortly by the rattle of wheels and the clink of horses' hoofs.

"Now, Watson," said Holmes, as a tall dog-cart dashed up through the gloom, throwing out two golden tunnels of yellow light from its side lanterns. "You'll come with me, won't you?

"If I can be of use."

"Oh, a trusty comrade is always of use; and a chronicler still more so. My room at The Cedars is a double-bedded one."

"The Cedars?"

"Yes; that is Mr. St. Clair's house. I am staying there while I conduct the inquiry."

"Where is it, then?"

"Near Lee, in Kent. We have a seven-mile drive before us."

"But I am all in the dark."

"Of course you are. You'll know all about it presently. Jump up here. All right, John; we shall not need you. Here's half a crown. Look out for me to-morrow, about eleven. Give her her head. So long, then!"

He flicked the horse with his whip, and we dashed away through the endless succession of somber and deserted streets, which widened gradually, until we were flying across a broad balustraded bridge, with the murky river flowing sluggishly beneath us. Beyond lay another dull wilderness of bricks and mortar, its silence broken only by the heavy, regular footfall of the policeman, or the songs and shouts of some belated party of revellers. A dull wrack was drifting slowly across the sky, and a star or two twinkled dimly here and there through the rifts of the clouds. Holmes drove in silence, with his head sunk upon his breast, and the air of a man who is lost in thought, while I sat beside him, curious to learn what this new quest might be which seemed to tax his powers so sorely, and yet afraid to break in upon the current of his thoughts. We had driven several miles, and were beginning to get to the fringe of the belt of suburban villas, when he shook himself, shrugged his shoulders, and lit up his pipe with the air of a man who has satisfied himself that he is acting for the best.

"You have a grand gift of silence, Watson," said he. "It makes you quite invaluable as a companion. 'Pon my word, it is a great thing for me to have someone to talk to, for my own thoughts are not over-pleasant. I was wondering what I should say to this dear little woman to-night when she meets me at the door."

"You forget that I know nothing about it."

"I shall just have time to tell you the facts of the case before we get to Lee. It seems absurdly simple, and yet, somehow I can get nothing to go upon. There's plenty of thread, no doubt, but I can't get the end of it into my hand. Now, I'll state the case clearly and concisely to you, Watson, and maybe you can see a spark where all is dark to me."

"Proceed, then."

"Some years ago — to be definite, in May, 1884 — there came to Lee a gentleman, Neville St. Clair by name, who appeared to have plenty of money. He took a large villa, laid out the grounds very nicely, and lived generally in good style. By degrees he made friends in the neighborhood, and in 1887 he married the daughter of a local brewer, by whom he now has two children. He had no occupation, but was interested in several companies and went into town as a rule in the morning, returning by the 5:14 from Cannon Street every night. Mr. St. Clair is now thirty-seven years of age, is a man of temperate habits, a good husband, a very affectionate father, and a man who is popular with all who know him. I may add that his whole debts at the present moment, as far as we have been able to ascertain amount to 88 pounds 10s., while he has 220 pounds standing to his credit in the Capital and Counties Bank. There is no reason, therefore, to think that money troubles have been weighing upon his mind.

"Last Monday Mr. Neville St. Clair went into town rather earlier than usual, remarking before he started that he had two important commissions to perform, and that he would bring his little boy home a box of bricks. Now, by the merest chance, his wife received a telegram upon this same Monday, very shortly after his departure, to the effect that a small parcel of considerable value which she had been expecting was waiting for her at the offices of the Aberdeen Shipping Company. Now, if you are well up in your London, you will know that the office of the company is in Fresno Street, which branches out of Upper Swandam Lane, where you found me to-night. Mrs. St. Clair had her lunch, started for the City, did some shopping, proceeded to the company's office, got her packet, and found herself at exactly 4:35 walking through Swandam Lane on her way back to the station. Have you followed me so far?"

"It is very clear."

"If you remember, Monday was an exceedingly hot day, and Mrs. St. Clair walked slowly, glancing about in the hope of seeing a cab, as she did not like the neighborhood in which she found herself. While she was walking in this way down Swandam Lane, she suddenly heard an ejaculation or cry, and was struck cold to see her husband looking down at her and, as it seemed to her, beckoning to her from a second-floor window. The window was open, and she distinctly saw his face, which she describes as being terribly agitated. He waved his hands frantically to her, and then vanished from the window so suddenly that it seemed to her that he had been plucked back by some irresistible force from behind. One singular point which struck her quick feminine eye was that although he wore some dark coat, such as he had started to town in, he had on neither collar nor necktie.

"Convinced that something was amiss with him, she rushed down the steps — for the house was none other than the opium den in which you found me to-night — and running through the front room she attempted to ascend the stairs which led to the first floor. At the foot of the stairs, however, she met this Lascar scoundrel of whom I have spoken, who thrust her back and, aided by a Dane, who acts as assistant there, pushed her out into the street. Filled with the most maddening doubts and fears, she rushed down the lane and, by rare good-fortune, met in Fresno Street a number of constables with an inspector, all on their way to their beat. The inspector and two men accompanied her back, and in spite of the continued resistance of the proprietor, they made their way to the room in which Mr. St. Clair had last been seen. There was no sign of him there. In fact, in the whole of that floor there was no one to be found save a crippled wretch of hideous aspect, who, it seems, made his home there. Both he and the Lascar stoutly swore that no one else had been in the front room during the afternoon. So determined was their denial that the inspector was staggered, and had almost come to believe that Mrs. St. Clair had been deluded when, with a cry, she sprang at a small deal box which lay upon the table and tore the lid from it. Out there fell a cascade of children's bricks. It was the toy which he had promised to bring home.

"This discovery, and the evident confusion which the cripple showed, made the inspector realize that the matter was serious. The rooms were carefully examined, and results all pointed to an abominable crime. The front room was plainly furnished as a sitting-room and led into a small bedroom, which looked out upon the back of one of the wharves. Between the wharf and the bedroom window is a narrow strip, which is dry at low tide but is covered at high tide with at least four and a half feet of water. The bedroom window was a broad one and opened from below. On examination traces of blood were to be seen upon the windowsill, and several scattered drops were visible upon the wooden floor of the bedroom. Thrust away behind a curtain in the front room were all the clothes of Mr. Neville St. Clair, with the exception of his coat. His boots, his socks, his hat, and his watch — all were there. There were no signs of violence upon any of these garments, and there were no other traces of Mr. Neville St. Clair. Out of the window he must apparently have gone for no other exit could be discovered, and the ominous bloodstains upon the sill gave little promise that he could save himself by swimming, for the tide was at its very highest at the moment of the tragedy.

"And now as to the villains who seemed to be immediately implicated in the matter. The Lascar was known to be a man of the vilest antecedents, but as, by Mrs. St. Clair's story, he was known to have been at the foot of the stair within a very few seconds of her husband's appearance at the window, he could hardly have been more than an accessory to the crime. His defense was one of absolute ignorance, and he protested that he had no knowledge as to the doings of Hugh Boone, his lodger, and that he could not account in any way for the presence of the missing gentleman's clothes.

"So much for the Lascar manager. Now for the sinister cripple who lives upon the second floor of the opium den, and who was certainly the last human being whose eyes rested upon Neville St. Clair. His name is Hugh Boone, and his hideous face is one which is familiar to every man who goes much to the City. He is a professional beggar, though in order to avoid the police regulations he pretends to a small trade in wax vestas. Some little distance down Threadneedle Street, upon the left-hand side, there is, as you may have remarked, a small angle in the wall. Here it is that this creature takes his daily seat, cross-legged with his tiny stock of matches on his lap, and as he is a piteous spectacle a small rain of charity descends into the greasy leather cap which lies upon the pavement beside him. I have watched the fellow more than once before ever I thought of making his professional acquaintance, and I have been surprised at the harvest which he has reaped in a short time. His appearance, you see, is so remarkable that no one can pass him without observing him. A shock of orange hair, a pale face disfigured by a horrible scar, which, by its contraction, has turned up the outer edge of his upper lip, a bulldog chin, and a pair of very penetrating dark eyes, which present a singular contrast to the color of his hair, all mark him out from amid the common crowd of mendicants and so, too, does his wit, for he is ever ready with a reply to any piece of chaff which may be thrown at him by the passers-by. This is the man whom we now learn to have been the lodger at the opium den, and to have been the last man to see the gentleman of whom we are in quest."

"But a cripple!" said I. "What could he have done single-handed against a man in the prime of life?"

"He is a cripple in the sense that he walks with a limp; but in other respects he appears to be a powerful and well-nurtured man. Surely your medical experience would tell you, Watson, that weakness in one limb is often compensated for by exceptional strength in the others."

"Pray continue your narrative."

"Mrs. St. Clair had fainted at the sight of the blood upon the window, and she was escorted home in a cab by the police, as her presence could be of no help to them in their investigations. Inspector Barton, who had charge of the case, made a very careful examination of the premises, but without finding anything which threw any light upon the matter. One mistake had been made in not arresting Boone instantly, as he was allowed some few minutes during which he might have communicated with his friend the Lascar, but this fault was soon remedied, and he was seized and searched, without anything being found which could incriminate him. There were, it is true, some blood-stains upon his right shirt-sleeve, but he pointed to his ring-finger, which had been cut near the nail, and explained that the bleeding came from there, adding that he had been to the window not long before, and that the stains which had been observed there came doubtless from the same source. He denied strenuously having ever seen Mr. Neville St. Clair and swore that the presence of the clothes in his room was as much a mystery to him as to the police. As to Mrs. St. Clair's assertion that she had actually seen her husband at the window, he declared that she must have been either mad or dreaming. He was removed, loudly protesting, to the police-station, while the inspector remained upon the premises in the hope that the ebbing tide might afford some fresh clew.

"And it did, though they hardly found upon the mud-bank what they had feared to find. It was Neville St. Clair's coat, and not Neville St. Clair, which lay uncovered as the tide receded. And what do you think they found in the pockets?"

"I cannot imagine."

"No, I don't think you would guess. Every pocket stuffed with pennies and half-pennies — 421 pennies and 270 half-pennies. It was no wonder that it had not been swept away by the tide. But a human body is a different matter. There is a fierce eddy between the wharf and the house. It seemed likely enough that the weighted coat had remained when the stripped body had been sucked away into the river."

"But I understand that all the other clothes were found in the room. Would the body be dressed in a coat alone?"

"No, sir, but the facts might be met speciously enough. Suppose that this man Boone had thrust Neville St. Clair through the window, there is no human eye which could have seen the deed. What would he do then? It would of course instantly strike him that he must get rid of the tell-tale garments. He would seize the coat, then, and be in the act of throwing it out, when it would occur to him that it would swim and not sink. He has little time, for he has heard the scuffle downstairs when the wife tried to force her way up, and perhaps he has already heard from his Lascar confederate that the police are hurrying up the street. There is not an instant to be lost. He rushes to some secret hoard, where he has accumulated the fruits of his beggary, and he stuffs all the coins upon which he can lay his hands into the pockets to make sure of the coat's sinking. He throws it out, and would have done the same with the other garments had not he heard the rush of steps below, and only just had time to close the window when the police appeared."

"It certainly sounds feasible."

"Well, we will take it as a working hypothesis for want of a better. Boone, as I have told you, was arrested and taken to the station, but it could not be shown that there had ever before been anything against him. He had for years been known as a professional beggar, but his life appeared to have been a very quiet and innocent one. There the matter stands at present, and the questions which have to be solved — what Neville St. Clair was doing in the opium den, what happened to him when there, where is he now, and what Hugh Boone had to do with his disappearance — are all as far from a solution as ever. I confess that I cannot recall any case within my experience which looked at the first glance so simple and yet which presented such difficulties."

While Sherlock Holmes had been detailing this singular series of events, we had been whirling through the outskirts of the great town until the last straggling houses had been left behind, and we rattled along with a country hedge upon either side of us. Just as he finished, however, we drove through two scattered villages, where a few lights still glimmered in the windows.

"We are on the outskirts of Lee," said my companion. "We have touched on three English counties in our short drive, starting in Middlesex, passing over an angle of Surrey, and ending in Kent. See that light among the trees? That is The Cedars, and beside that lamp sits a woman whose anxious ears have already, I have little doubt, caught the clink of our horse's feet."

"But why are you not conducting the case from Baker Street?" I asked.

"Because there are many inquiries which must be made out here. Mrs. St. Clair has most kindly put two rooms at my disposal, and you may rest assured that she will have nothing but a welcome for my friend and colleague. I hate to meet her, Watson, when I have no news of her husband. Here we are. Whoa, there, whoa!"

We had pulled up in front of a large villa which stood within its own grounds. A stable-boy had run out to the horse's head, and springing down, I followed Holmes up the small, winding gravel-drive which led to the house. As we approached, the door flew open, and a little blonde woman stood in the opening, clad in some sort of light mousseline de soie, with a touch of fluffy pink chiffon at her neck and wrists. She stood with her figure outlined against the flood of light, one hand upon the door, one half-raised in her eagerness, her body slightly bent, her head and face protruded, with eager eyes and parted lips, a standing question.

"Well?" she cried, "well?" And then, seeing that there were two of us, she gave a cry of hope which sank into a groan as she saw that my companion shook his head and shrugged his shoulders.

"No good news?"

"None."

"No bad?"

"No."

"Thank God for that. But come in. You must be weary, for you have had a long day."

"This is my friend, Dr. Watson. He has been of most vital use to me in several of my cases, and a lucky chance has made it possible for me to bring him out and associate him with this investigation."

"I am delighted to see you," said she, pressing my hand warmly. "You will, I am sure, forgive anything that may be wanting in our arrangements, when you consider the blow which has come so suddenly upon us."

"My dear madam," said I, "I am an old campaigner, and if I were not I can very well see that no apology is needed. If I can be of any assistance, either to you or to my friend here, I shall be indeed happy."

"Now, Mr. Sherlock Holmes," said the lady as we entered a well-lit dining-room, upon the table of which a cold supper had been laid out, "I should very much like to ask you one or two plain questions, to which I beg that you will give a plain answer."

"Certainly, madam."

"Do not trouble about my feelings. I am not hysterical, nor given to fainting. I simply wish to hear your real, real opinion."

"Upon what point?"

"In your heart of hearts, do you think that Neville is alive?"

Sherlock Holmes seemed to be embarrassed by the question. "Frankly, now!" she repeated, standing upon the rug and looking keenly down at him as he leaned back in a basket-chair.

"Frankly, then, madam, I do not."

"You think that he is dead?"

"I do."

"Murdered?"

"I don't say that. Perhaps."

"And on what day did he meet his death?"

"On Monday."

"Then perhaps, Mr. Holmes, you will be good enough to explain how it is that I have received a letter from him to-day."

Sherlock Holmes sprang out of his chair as if he had been galvanized.

"What!" he roared.

"Yes, to-day." She stood smiling, holding up a little slip of paper in the air.

"May I see it?"

"Certainly."

He snatched it from her in his eagerness, and smoothing it out upon the table he drew over the lamp and examined it intently. I had left my chair and was gazing at it over his shoulder. The envelope was a very coarse one and was stamped with the Gravesend postmark and with the date of that very day, or rather of the day before, for it was considerably after midnight.

"Coarse writing," murmured Holmes. "Surely this is not your husband's writing, madam."

"No, but the enclosure is."

"I perceive also that whoever addressed the envelope had to go and inquire as to the address."

"How can you tell that?"

"The name, you see, is in perfectly black ink, which has dried itself. The rest is of the grayish color, which shows that blotting-paper has been used. If it had been written straight off, and then blotted, none would be of a deep black shade. This man has written the name, and there has then been a pause before he wrote the address, which can only mean that he was not familiar with it. It is, of course, a trifle, but there is nothing so important as trifles. Let us now see the letter. Ha! there has been an enclosure here!"

"Yes, there was a ring. His signet-ring."

"And you are sure that this is your husband's hand?"

"One of his hands."

"One?"

"His hand when he wrote hurriedly. It is very unlike his usual writing, and yet I know it well."

"'Dearest do not be frightened. All will come well. There is a huge error which it may take some little time to rectify. Wait in patience. — NEVILLE.' Written in pencil upon the fly-leaf of a book, octavo size, no water-mark. Hum! Posted to-day in Gravesend by a man with a dirty thumb. Ha! And the flap has been gummed, if I am not very much in error, by a person who had been chewing tobacco. And you have no doubt that it is your husband's hand, madam?"

"None. Neville wrote those words."

"And they were posted to-day at Gravesend. Well, Mrs. St. Clair, the clouds lighten, though I should not venture to say that the danger is over."

"But he must be alive, Mr. Holmes."

"Unless this is a clever forgery to put us on the wrong scent. The ring, after all, proves nothing. It may have been taken from him.'

"No, no; it is, it is his very own writing!"

"Very well. It may, however, have been written on Monday and only posted to-day."

"That is possible."

"If so, much may have happened between."

"Oh, you must not discourage me, Mr. Holmes. I know that all is well with him. There is so keen a sympathy between us that I should know if evil came upon him. On the very day that I saw him last he cut himself in the bedroom, and yet I in the dining-room rushed upstairs instantly with the utmost certainty that something had happened. Do you think that I would respond to such a trifle and yet be ignorant of his death?"

"I have seen too much not to know that the impression of a woman may be more valuable than the conclusion of an analytical reasoner. And in this letter you certainly have a very strong piece of evidence to corroborate your view. But if your husband is alive and able to write letters, why should he remain away from you?"

"I cannot imagine. It is unthinkable."

"And on Monday he made no remarks before leaving you?"

"No."

"And you were surprised to see him in Swandam Lane?"

"Very much so."

"Was the window open?"

"Yes."

"Then he might have called to you?"

"He might."

"He only, as I understand, gave an inarticulate cry?"

"Yes."

"A call for help, you thought?"

"Yes. He waved his hands."

"But it might have been a cry of surprise. Astonishment at the unexpected sight of you might cause him to throw up his hands?"

"It is possible."

"And you thought he was pulled back?"

"He disappeared so suddenly."

"He might have leaped back. You did not see anyone else in the room?"

"No, but this horrible man confessed to having been there, and the Lascar was at the foot of the stairs."

"Quite so. Your husband, as far as you could see, had his ordinary clothes on?"

"But without his collar or tie. I distinctly saw his bare throat."

"Had he ever spoken of Swandam Lane?"

"Never."

"Had he ever showed any signs of having taken opium?"

"Never."

"Thank you, Mrs. St. Clair. Those are the principal points about which I wished to be absolutely clear. We shall now have a little supper and then retire, for we may have a very busy day to-morrow."

A large and comfortable double-bedded room had been placed at our disposal, and I was quickly between the sheets, for I was weary after my night of adventure. Sherlock Holmes was a man, however, who, when he had an unsolved problem upon his mind, would go for days, and even for a week, without rest, turning it over, rearranging his facts, looking at it from every point of view until he had either fathomed it or convinced himself that his data were insufficient. It was soon evident to me that he was now preparing for an all-night sitting. He took off his coat and waistcoat, put on a large blue dressing-gown, and then wandered about the room collecting pillows from his bed and cushions from the sofa and armchairs. With these he constructed a sort of Eastern divan, upon which he perched himself cross-legged, with an ounce of shag tobacco and a box of matches laid out in front of him. In the dim light of the lamp I saw him sitting there, an old briar pipe between his lips, his eyes fixed vacantly upon the corner of the ceiling, the blue smoke curling up from him, silent, motionless, with the light shining upon his strong-set aquiline features. So he sat as I dropped off to sleep, and so he sat when a sudden ejaculation caused me to wake up, and I found the summer sun shining into the apartment. The pipe was still between his lips, the smoke still curled upward, and the room was full of a dense tobacco haze, but nothing remained of the heap of shag which I had seen upon the previous night.

"Awake, Watson?" he asked.

"Yes."

"Game for a morning drive?"

"Certainly."

"Then dress. No one is stirring yet, but I know where the stable-boy sleeps, and we shall soon have the trap out." He chuckled to himself as he spoke, his eyes twinkled, and he seemed a different man to the somber thinker of the previous night.

As I dressed I glanced at my watch. It was no wonder that no one was stirring. It was twenty-five minutes past four. I had hardly finished when Holmes returned with the news that the boy was putting in the horse.

"I want to test a little theory of mine," said he, pulling on his boots. "I think, Watson, that you are now standing in the presence of one of the most absolute fools in Europe. I deserve to be kicked from here to Charing Cross. But I think I have the key of the affair now."

"And where is it?" I asked, smiling.

"In the bathroom," he answered. "Oh, yes, I am not joking," he continued, seeing my look of incredulity. "I have just been there, and I have taken it out, and I have got it in this Gladstone bag. Come on, my boy, and we shall see whether it will not fit the lock."

We made our way downstairs as quietly as possible, and out into the bright morning sunshine. In the road stood our horse and trap, with the half-clad stable-boy waiting at the head. We both sprang in, and away we dashed down the London Road. A few country carts were stirring, bearing in vegetables to the metropolis, but the lines of villas on either side were as silent and lifeless as some city in a dream.

"It has been in some points a singular case," said Holmes, flicking the horse on into a gallop. "I confess that I have been as blind as a mole, but it is better to learn wisdom late than never to learn it at all."

In town the earliest risers were just beginning to look sleepily from their windows as we drove through the streets of the Surrey side. Passing down the Waterloo Bridge Road we crossed over the river, and dashing up Wellington Street wheeled sharply to the right and found ourselves in Bow Street. Sherlock Holmes was well known to the force, and the two constables at the door saluted him. One of them held the horse's head while the other led us in.

"Who is on duty?" asked Holmes.

"Inspector Bradstreet, sir."

"Ah, Bradstreet, how are you?" A tall, stout official had come down the stone-flagged passage, in a peaked cap and frogged jacket. "I wish to have a quiet word with you, Bradstreet." "Certainly, Mr. Holmes. Step into my room here." It was a small, office-like room, with a huge ledger upon the table, and a telephone projecting from the wall. The inspector sat down at his desk.

"What can I do for you, Mr. Holmes?"

"I called about that beggarman, Boone — the one who was charged with being concerned in the disappearance of Mr. Neville St. Clair, of Lee."

"Yes. He was brought up and remanded for further inquiries."

"So I heard. You have him here?"

"In the cells."

"Is he quiet?"

"Oh, he gives no trouble. But he is a dirty scoundrel."

"Dirty?"

"Yes, it is all we can do to make him wash his hands, and his face is as black as a tinker's. Well, when once his case has been settled, he will have a regular prison bath; and I think, if you saw him, you would agree with me that he needed it."

"I should like to see him very much."

"Would you? That is easily done. Come this way. You can leave your bag."

"No, I think that I'll take it."

"Very good. Come this way, if you please." He led us down a passage, opened a barred door, passed down a winding stair, and brought us to a whitewashed corridor with a line of doors on each side.

"The third on the right is his," said the inspector. "Here it is!" He quietly shot back a panel in the upper part of the door and glanced through.

"He is asleep," said he. "You can see him very well."

We both put our eyes to the grating. The prisoner lay with his face towards us, in a very deep sleep, breathing slowly and heavily. He was a middle-sized man, coarsely clad as became his calling, with a colored shirt protruding through the rent in his tattered coat. He was, as the inspector had said, extremely dirty, but the grime which covered his face could not conceal its repulsive ugliness. A broad wheal from an old scar ran right across it from eye to chin, and by its contraction had turned up one side of the upper lip, so that three teeth were exposed in a perpetual snarl. A shock of very bright red hair grew low over his eyes and forehead.

"He's a beauty, isn't he?" said the inspector.

"He certainly needs a wash," remarked Holmes. "I had an idea that he might, and I took the liberty of bringing the tools with me." He opened the Gladstone bag as he spoke, and took out, to my astonishment, a very large bath-sponge.

"He! he! You are a funny one," chuckled the inspector.

"Now, if you will have the great goodness to open that door very quietly, we will soon make him cut a much more respectable figure."

"Well, I don't know why not," said the inspector. "He doesn't look a credit to the Bow Street cells, does he?" He slipped his key into the lock, and we all very quietly entered the cell. The sleeper half turned, and then settled down once more into a deep slumber. Holmes stooped to the waterjug, moistened his sponge, and then rubbed it twice vigorously across and down the prisoner's face.

"Let me introduce you," he shouted, "to Mr. Neville St. Clair, of Lee, in the county of Kent."

Never in my life have I seen such a sight. The man's face peeled off under the sponge like the bark from a tree. Gone was the coarse brown tint! Gone, too, was the horrid scar which had seamed it across, and the twisted lip which had given the repulsive sneer to the face! A twitch brought away the tangled red hair, and there, sitting up in his bed, was a pale, sad-faced, refined-looking man, black-haired and smooth-skinned, rubbing his eyes and staring about him with sleepy bewilderment. Then suddenly realizing the exposure, he broke into a scream and threw himself down with his face to the pillow.

"Great heavens!" cried the inspector, "it is, indeed, the missing man. I know him from the photograph."

The prisoner turned with the reckless air of a man who abandons himself to his destiny. "Be it so," said he. "And pray what am I charged with?"

"With making away with Mr. Neville St.-Oh, come, you can't be charged with that unless they make a case of attempted suicide of it," said the inspector with a grin. "Well, I have been twenty-seven years in the force, but this really takes the cake."

"If I am Mr. Neville St. Clair, then it is obvious that no crime has been committed, and that, therefore, I am illegally detained."

"No crime, but a very great error has been committed," said Holmes. "You would have done better to have trusted you wife."

"It was not the wife; it was the children," groaned the prisoner. "God help me, I would not have them ashamed of their father. My God! What an exposure! What can I do?"

Sherlock Holmes sat down beside him on the couch and patted him kindly on the shoulder.

"If you leave it to a court of law to clear the matter up," said he, "of course you can hardly avoid publicity. On the other hand, if you convince the police authorities that there is no possible case against you, I do not know that there is any reason that the details should find their way into the papers. Inspector Bradstreet would, I am sure, make notes upon anything which you might tell us and submit it to the proper authorities. The case would then never go into court at all."

"God bless you!" cried the prisoner passionately. "I would have endured imprisonment, ay, even execution, rather than have left my miserable secret as a family blot to my children.

"You are the first who have ever heard my story. My father was a school-master in Chesterfield, where I received an excellent education. I travelled in my youth, took to the stage, and finally became a reporter on an evening paper in London. One day my editor wished to have a series of articles upon begging in the metropolis, and I volunteered to supply them. There was the point from which all my adventures started. It was only by trying begging as an amateur that I could get the facts upon which to base my articles. When an actor I had, of course, learned all the secrets of making up, and had been famous in the greenroom for my skill. I took advantage now of my attainments. I painted my face, and to make myself as pitiable as possible I made a good scar and fixed one side of my lip in a twist by the aid of a small slip of flesh-colored plaster. Then with a red head of hair, and an appropriate dress, I took my station in the business part of the city, ostensibly as a match-seller but really as a beggar. For seven hours I plied my trade, and when I returned home in the evening I found to my surprise that I had received no less than 26s. 4d.

"I wrote my articles and thought little more of the matter until, some time later, I backed a bill for a friend and had a writ served upon me for 25 pounds. I was at my wit's end where to get the money, but a sudden idea came to me. I begged a fortnight's grace from the creditor, asked for a holiday from my employers, and spent the time in begging in the City under my disguise. In ten days I had the money and had paid the debt.

"Well, you can imagine how hard it was to settle down to arduous work at 2 pounds a week when I knew that I could earn as much in a day by smearing my face with a little paint, laying my cap on the ground, and sitting still. It was a long fight between my pride and the money, but the dollars won at last, and I threw up reporting and sat day after day in the corner which I had first chosen, inspiring pity by my ghastly face and filling my pockets with coppers. Only one man knew my secret. He was the keeper of a low den in which I used to lodge in Swandam Lane, where I could every morning emerge as a squalid beggar and in the evenings transform myself into a well-dressed man about town. This fellow, a Lascar, was well paid by me for his rooms, so that I knew that my secret was safe in his possession.

"Well, very soon I found that I was saving considerable sums of money. I do not mean that any beggar in the streets of London could earn 700 pounds a year — which is less than my average takings — but I had exceptional advantages in my power of making up, and also in a facility of repartee, which improved by practice and made me quite a recognized character in the City. All day a stream of pennies, varied by silver, poured in upon me, and it was a very bad day in which I failed to take 2 pounds.

"As I grew richer I grew more ambitious, took a house in the country, and eventually married, without anyone having a suspicion as to my real occupation. My dear wife knew that I had business in the City. She little knew what.

"Last Monday I had finished for the day and was dressing in my room above the opium den when I looked out of my window and saw, to my horror and astonishment, that my wife was standing in the street, with her eyes fixed full upon me. I gave a cry of surprise, threw up my arms to cover my face, and, rushing to my confidant, the Lascar, entreated him to prevent anyone from coming up to me. I heard her voice downstairs, but I knew that she could not ascend. Swiftly I threw off my clothes, pulled on those of a beggar, and put on my pigments and wig. Even a wife's eyes could not pierce so complete a disguise. But then it occurred to me that there might be a search in the room, and that the clothes might betray me. I threw open the window, reopening by my violence a small cut which I had inflicted upon myself in the bedroom that morning. Then I seized my coat, which was weighted by the coppers which I had just transferred to it from the leather bag in which I carried my takings. I hurled it out of the window, and it disappeared into the Thames. The other clothes would have followed, but at that moment there was a rush of constables up the stair, and a few minutes after I found, rather, I confess, to my relief, that instead of being identified as Mr. Neville St. Clair, I was arrested as his murderer.

"I do not know that there is anything else for me to explain. I was determined to preserve my disguise as long as possible, and hence my preference for a dirty face. Knowing that my wife would be terribly anxious, I slipped off my ring and confided it to the Lascar at a moment when no constable was watching me, together with a hurried scrawl, telling her that she had no cause to fear."

"That note only reached her yesterday," said Holmes.

"Good God! What a week she must have spent!"

"The police have watched this Lascar," said Inspector Bradstreet, "and I can quite understand that he might find it difficult to post a letter unobserved. Probably he handed it to some sailor customer of his, who forgot all about it for some days."

"That was it," said Holmes, nodding approvingly; "I have no doubt of it. But have you never been prosecuted for begging?"

"Many times; but what was a fine to me?"

"It must stop here, however," said Bradstreet. "If the police are to hush this thing up, there must be no more of Hugh Boone."

"I have sworn it by the most solemn oaths which a man can take."

"In that case I think that it is probable that no further steps may be taken. But if you are found again, then all must come out. I am sure, Mr. Holmes, that we are very much indebted to you for having cleared the matter up. I wish I knew how you reach your results."

"I reached this one," said my friend, "by sitting upon five pillows and consuming an ounce of shag. I think, Watson, that if we drive to Baker Street we shall just be in time for breakfast."

Made in United States
North Haven, CT
10 June 2022